The's amazing, Steve!

What's, Steve?

I didn't know you could make bananas magnetic.

Neither did John Watt until he met mad boy scientist, Vernon Bright.

How does he magnetize a banana?

You could say he bends the laws of physics. And after that he gets stuck with some pretty mad characters.

You mean they're a wild bunch?

Yeah. Of course, Vernie has a magnetic personality - and a magnetic body, as it happens.

I suppose he attracts trouble.

You're not kidding! You know what happens to people who monkey around with bananas?

No, what?

They slip up.

I hope there're better jokes than that in the book.

You'll just have to read it and find out.

About the authors

Steve Barlow is tall and hairy. Steve Skidmore isn't.

They have written quite a few books together. Barlow does the vowels, Skidmore does the consonants. They generally leave the punctuation to sort itself out. They like writing, especially when it gets them out of doing the shopping, the ironing or the washing up.

Their other Puffin books include the *Mad Myths* series, which they say is fast, furious, fantastic and frightfully silly.

You can find out more about Steve Barlow and Steve Skidmore on the Web. Visit them at www.puffin.co.uk

Some other books by
Steve Barlow and Steve Skidmore

VERNON BRIGHT AND
FRANKENSTEIN'S HAMSTER

VERNON BRIGHT AND
THE FASTER-THAN-LIGHT SHOW

MAD MYTHS: STONE ME!
MAD MYTHS: MIND THE DOOR!
MAD MYTHS: A TOUCH OF WIND!
MAD MYTHS: MUST FLY!

STEVE BARLOW AND STEVE SKIDMORE

Vernon Bright and

THE MAGNETIC BANANA

Illustrated by
GEO PARKIN

PUFFIN BOOKS

PUFFIN BOOKS

Penguin Books Ltd, 27 Wrights Lane, London W8 5TZ, England
Penguin Putnam Inc., 375 Hudson Street, New York, New York 10014, USA
Penguin Books Australia Ltd, Ringwood, Victoria, Australia
Penguin Books Canada Ltd, 10 Alcorn Avenue, Toronto, Ontario, Canada M4V 3B2
Penguin Books India (P) Ltd, 11 Community Centre, Panchsheel Park, New Delhi – 110 017, India
Penguin Books (NZ) Ltd, Cnr Rosedale and Airborne Roads, Albany, Auckland, New Zealand
Penguin Books (South Africa) (Pty) Ltd, 5 Watkins Street, Denver Ext 4,
Johannesburg 2094, South Africa

On the World Wide Web at: www.penguin.com

Penguin Books Ltd, Registered Offices: Harmondsworth, Middlesex, England

First published 2000
4

Text copyright © Steve Barlow and Steve Skidmore, 2000
Illustrations copyright © Geo Parkin, 2000
All rights reserved

The moral right of the author and illustrator has been asserted

Set in 12½/18 Palatino

Made and printed in England by Clays Ltd, St Ives plc

British Library Cataloguing in Publication Data
A CIP catalogue record for this book is available from the British Library

ISBN 0–141–30584–3

CONTENTS

The two Steves would like to thank Trevor Day for his invaluable advice on the scientific principles referred to in this book, and for pointing out which of our ideas were 'come on, boys, that's totally impossible,' and which were merely 'completely gaga, but what the heck, it's sci-fi'. Any remaining inaccuracies are what we managed to slip in while he was looking the other way.

Caution: this book was written under carefully controlled conditions, supervised by safety experts. Turning bananas into magnets is highly dangerous and readers should not try to do this at home.

CHAPTER ONE

'Science!' groaned John Watt. 'I hate science.'

John was standing outside a grim-looking brown door. Through the layers of age-old paint, the words *'Science Laboratory 1'* were just about visible to the naked eye. The writing was done in faded gold and old-fashioned letters. Frankenstein's laboratory probably had a sign just like it. John squinted at his new timetable to check he was in the right place at the right time. He hoped he'd got it wrong. He hadn't.

– ELMLEY SCHOOL –

MONDAY, PERIOD ONE: Science – Mr Allen
in Science Lab 1

Science! It wasn't much of an incentive to wake up on a Monday morning, thought John. He couldn't quite picture himself leaping out of bed at the crack of dawn yelling, 'Oh yippee, thank goodness the weekend's over, I must rush to school to get to my science lesson!' Although, thinking about it, John couldn't picture himself leaping out of bed at the crack of dawn on any morning. Going to school wasn't an incentive to get out of bed, full stop. Especially going to a new school where he didn't know anyone.

John stood for a moment, thinking about what future diseases and illnesses he could try to convince his mother he had caught in order to avoid:

a) Science on a Monday morning and

b) School, on every other morning . . .

Mumps, flu, veruccas and bubonic plague sprang to mind, but he knew his mum would just say something like, 'Really, dear, you've caught bubonic plague? Oh, how terrible for you. Well, off you go to school and I hope you don't die.'

Eventually, John summoned up his courage, knocked on the door and entered the lab.

'Yes?'

John assumed the strange-looking figure standing at the front of the lab, pointing at some meaningless squiggles on a whiteboard, was Mr Allen, Teacher of Science, Elmley School, Monday, period one.

'I'm new,' squeaked John. 'It's my first day.'

Mr Allen peered over his half-rim glasses.

'A new student in the summer term? Hmm, I wasn't told about this. But of course, they never tell me anything, I'm always the last to know. Not like the old days, not when I was doing the timetable . . .'

John stood still, wondering what he should do as Mr Allen continued grumbling to himself. John was aware that the class was staring at him. He began to fidget.

Mr Allen stopped muttering and fixed John with a stare. 'Not your fault, I suppose. Your name?'

'Watt,' said John.

'Your name?' repeated Mr Allen.

'Watt,' repeated John.

'Are you deaf?' Mr Allen grunted. 'What's your name?'

'That's right.'

'What's right?' Mr Allen looked bemused.

'Yes, it is,' said John, smiling encouragingly.

'What is?'

'Watt is,' explained John helpfully, or so he thought. Some of the class began to giggle.

Mr Allen stared hard at John. A flush of red began to travel up his neck and into his cheeks. 'Your first day and you're being rude to a teacher?'

John was confused. Being rude? He wasn't being rude. 'I'm not,' he replied.

'Not what?' Mr Allen was beginning to twitch.

John took a deep breath. 'No, I *am* Watt.'

Mr Allen's red flush was rapidly shooting up his forehead. He's going to explode, thought John, I'd better try and stop this. But how? Luckily, his mouth took over from his brain and came up with the answer. 'My name is John Watt, sir,' John heard himself call out.

'Oh.' Mr Allen paused. The red flush began to retreat. 'Why didn't you say so?'

John stared at him. 'I did, sir. Lots of times.'

The flush started upwards again. 'Are you contradicting me?'

'No, sir!'

'I've got my eye on you, Watt. Sit down.' Mr Allen, breathing heavily, turned back to the board.

John glanced nervously at the rest of the class. From the dense undergrowth of gas taps, DC power connectors, curved laboratory taps, test tubes and beakers, a forest of faces loomed. Not one of them was familiar, and they were all staring at him. Judging and forming an opinion of him. Probably not a good one, thought John.

'Over there, get a move on!' Mr Allen's barked order brought John back to his senses. Mr Allen was pointing towards the back of the class where there was a boy sitting at a bench on his own.

John scuttled over. The forest of faces followed John on his brief journey, then obeyed Mr Allen's command to 'Look this way!' and turned back towards the whiteboard.

The boy sitting on his own looked up at John as if he wasn't sure it was worth the effort. He nodded towards the empty stool next to him to indicate where John should sit.

'I'm Bright,' he said.

What a bighead, thought John as he scrutinized his new neighbour. He looked fairly normal. Except for his hair. John had never seen anything like it. It stood out at every conceivable angle, and at a few that defied the known laws of geometry. It looked as though he'd been in a fight with a mad gorilla armed with several tubes of exploding hair gel.

John suddenly realized he was staring, so he nodded a half-hearted hello and sat down.

As he reached into his bag for his pencil case, he gave out a sigh. What a start! And all because of his name. Just like it had been at his old school. 'Watt's what?', 'Watt a laugh', 'Watt are you doing?', 'Watt's the answer?' If he'd heard the pun once, he'd heard it a million times.

In his innocence, John had thought that a new start would mean no more name trouble. That thought had been the only good thing about moving.

'We're going away,' his mum had said. 'A new town; a new job for me; a new school for you. A new start for us.'

John had wanted to tell his mum that he didn't want the new. The new scared him and, despite the teasing about his name, he was quite happy with the old, thank you very much. But when his dad had left home 'because things weren't working out' and his mum had decided that she and John needed a 'new start', John didn't have the heart to argue.

As his thoughts continued to drift, John was suddenly shocked back to the present as he heard Mr Allen's voice calling his name.

He sat bolt upright. 'Yes, sir?'

'What?' Mr Allen scowled.

'Yes, sir? Did you want me?' asked John, in all innocence.

'I wasn't talking to you!' snapped Mr Allen.

'But you said "Watt",' John said.

Mr Allen's flush returned with a vengeance. 'I wasn't talking to you and I didn't say "Watt", I said "what" to someone else who was asking a question, because I didn't hear what he was saying, Watt!' cried the exasperated teacher.

John's mind was reeling. 'What?'

'Don't start that again!' Mr Allen's flush had turned a nasty purple colour.

'Sorry,' mumbled John. He swore he could hear the sniggers of his new classmates.

Mr Allen rounded on John. 'Well, you obviously weren't paying attention. Can you tell me the subject matter with which we are dealing?'

John looked blank. He was in big trouble and he knew it.

'Units of electricity,' hissed the boy next to him.

'Units of electricity!' repeated John, glad of the lifeline that had been thrown him.

Mr Allen looked disappointed that John had been able to answer. 'Er, yes, correct. Units of electricity: the amp, the volt, the ohm and the watt ...' He pointed a quivering finger at John, *'and don't you dare say a word or you will live to regret it!'*

John sat and gawped at him.

'So,' said Mr Allen, through gritted teeth, 'let's see how much our new pupil knows.' The whole class turned to stare at John. He gulped.

Mr Allen growled, 'What's a watt, Watt?'

The class burst into gales of laughter. Mr Allen, realizing too late what he had just said, turned beetroot-coloured. As the classroom rocked with laughter, John felt a horrible urge to giggle creep over him. The feeling was quickly squashed and replaced by a huge stomach-churning spasm as Mr Allen turned his fury on the hapless newcomer.

'Watt!' roared Mr Allen. 'You're in detention!'

CHAPTER TWO

Bright Spark

As far as John was concerned, the rest of the science lesson passed in a blur. Amid the background bustle of the lesson, John was sure he could hear people making fun of his name.

'What's a Watt?', 'Who's Watt?', 'Which watt?' 'Watt a nitwit.'

It was all John could do to stop tears springing to his eyes.

Luckily, the school bell rang to signal the end of round one of John's ordeal. There was a mad scramble for the door, led by Mr Allen, who had an important meeting with a cup of coffee, a cream custard and two blood-pressure-reducing tablets.

The class quickly disappeared, leaving John

sitting in a swamp of misery. He felt stunned. His first lesson at his new school; he'd been given a detention and probably been judged a 'Mad Nutter Grade A' by the rest of the class. It couldn't have been a worse beginning if he'd tried!

'Don't worry about Mr Allen's detentions.'

John jumped. The boy with the exploded hair was still sitting next to him.

'He always forgets he's given them. He's famous for it,' the boy explained.

'Oh, thanks.' John's tonne of misery was lightened by a few grammes. He thought he'd better make conversation. 'What's your name?' he asked, trying to be cheery.

The boy raised his eyebrows. 'No. Watt's *your* name!'

A pained look passed over John's face.

'Don't worry, I'm in the same boat,' continued the boy breezily. 'My name gives me trouble as well.'

'Wh . . . and that is . . .?' said John, desperately trying to avoid the word 'what'.

'I told you earlier; I'm Bright. Vernon Bright, but I hate my first name so just call me Bright.'

The penny dropped. John laughed. 'Oh. Your

name is Bright. I thought you meant . . .' He tailed off in confusion.

Bright shrugged. 'Well, actually, even though I say it myself . . . I do take after my name.'

John tried to think of a joke to do with being clever and bright, but he couldn't. So instead he mumbled, 'Right, Bright.' Then realized what he'd said and groaned inwardly.

Bright, however, ignored the remark. 'Come on. It's maths next. And we can't be late for that. It's my second favourite lesson.'

Maths – second favourite lesson! Maths was John's second worst lesson after science. 'What's

your favourite lesson?' John asked, half guessing the answer.

'Science.'

No wonder Bright had been sitting alone at the desk, thought John as he followed his new companion through the maze of corridors. Anyone whose favourite lessons were science and maths *couldn't* be normal!

As they turned yet another corner, a crowd of older students came shooting towards them. The group saw Bright and slid to a halt. One of them pulled out a pair of sunglasses and put them on.

'I think I need these,' he sniggered, 'because it's *very bright*!'

The boy and his cronies burst into fits of laughter and continued down the corridor.

Bright glowered at the disappearing figures. 'One thousand, two hundred and seven!' he called after them. Turning back, he caught John's puzzled look.

'One thousand, two hundred and seven,' Bright explained, 'is the number of times this year that someone has made fun of my name. To my face, of course. I don't know what they say behind my back.'

John still looked blank. 'I don't get it.'

'My name is Vernon Bright,' said Bright.

John shrugged his shoulders. 'And . . . ?'

'My initial is V, which is often used as a shorthand way of writing "very".' Bright stared down the corridor and shouted pointedly, 'So certain *ignoramuses* think it's terribly amusing to call me "Very Bright". Ha ha!'

'Oh, I didn't think of that.' John began to chuckle. 'V. Bright, Very Bright! That's quite clever . . .' John stopped abruptly as his brain caught up with his mouth.

'One thousand, two hundred and eight,' muttered Bright.

John looked down at his feet. 'Sorry. I didn't mean to . . . you know . . .'

Bright sighed. 'I'll tell you what, Watt.' He shook his head. 'Look, you've got me doing it now. What I was going to say was, I think we should stick together. A kind of mutual support.' Bright held out his hand solemnly. 'What do you think, Watt?'

John thought for a moment, then shook the offered hand. 'I think it's a bright idea, Bright.'

A flicker of something crossed Bright's face. It

might have been a smile. He broke off the handshake and turned away abruptly.

John fell in behind.

Over the next few days, John spent most of his time at school with Bright. He sat with him in lessons and spent breaktimes chatting to him. This could be hard work. Chatting to Bright was like lobbing small pebbles into a large pool – the things John said caused very little disturbance and sank without trace. This was because Bright was only interested in talking about science, maths and electronics; all subjects John knew next to nothing about.

Bright was also pretty short-sighted when it came to spotting a joke. When John wondered why you could only ever find one of your socks in the morning when there'd been two there the night before, Bright scornfully dismissed John's Alien Sock Abduction Theory on the grounds that it was 'unscientific'.

John had taken a leaf out of Bright's book. He'd begun to keep count of the number of times people made puns and jokes about his name.

'I'm up to twenty-three,' he announced proudly towards the end of his first week at Elmley.

'That's nothing. I'm up to one thousand, two hundred and ninety-eight,' mused Bright. 'There's been a bit of a rush on the puns. It must be something in the air.'

John quickly discovered that Bright lived up to his name. He *was* bright. He always seemed to know the answers. He didn't always volunteer them, but somehow the slight smile on his face made it clear to everyone that he knew the answer even when he wasn't prepared to say what it was. This superior attitude clearly didn't improve his popularity with his classmates. It didn't seem to worry Bright that he wasn't popular. It would have worried John.

Bright's know-all attitude even extended to the teachers. During his next science lesson, Mr Allen was banging on about relativity (John thought this was something to do with aunts and uncles).

'. . . blah blah blah, Particle Wave Theory,' blathered Mr Allen, 'as developed by Einstein in his General Theory of Relativity in 1915, blah blah . . .'

Bright sat there shaking his head and muttering 'Codswallop', 'Utter rubbish', 'Nonsense' under his breath.

'What is?' asked John.

'Einstein developed his Particle Wave Theory in his Special Theory of Relativity, not the General Theory – and he wrote it in 1905, not 1915. Don't these teachers know *anything*?'

John was confused. You didn't argue with teachers, but Bright sounded very sure of his facts. Who was right? On the other hand, they were both talking double dutch, so who cared?

John's first PE lesson with Bright was a bit of an eye-opener. For some reason John had assumed that anyone who was fanatical about maths and science wouldn't like sport. They'd be too 'boffy' for that. He was wrong.

John's timetable hadn't given any details about the session, so he'd bought a complete collection of summer PE kit. His bag was full of cricket whites, trainers and athletic shorts.

'What are we actually doing?' John asked Bright as they stood in the changing rooms.

'Football,' answered Bright.

John looked skywards. He hadn't brought his boots. 'That's not a summer sport!' he complained.

'It's always football on Friday,' explained Bright.

'It doesn't matter what time of year it is, we always play football on Friday.'

'Come on, lads!' Mr Jones, the PE teacher bounded in. 'Friday afternoon football. Terrific!'

As he got changed, John was amazed to hear people not only talking to Bright, but actually being pleasant to him!

'I hope I'm in your team, Bright.'

'Hope I'm with you today.'

'Good luck, Bright, not that you need it!'

Bright just nodded and smiled at John who stood wondering what on earth was going on!

Outside, Mr Jones gathered the boys together on the pitch.

'Peters, Hoyle, captains. Hoyle, you choose first.'

Hoyle punched the air in joy as Peters cried out in protest, 'Sir, that's not fair! That means he'll get Bright.'

John looked on in astonishment as Bright lined up with Hoyle. Every time someone was chosen they either whooped with joy or looked downcast, depending on whether they were in Bright's team

or not. John had expected Bright to be picked last – or rather, second from last; he expected to be picked last himself. Half of John's prediction was spot on – he *was* picked last. However, he had the good fortune to be on the same side as Bright.

Mr Jones blew the whistle and the game began.

As he panted up and down the field, John couldn't work out why everyone had made such a fuss about Bright. He never tried to tackle, he didn't run; he just stood in the middle of the pitch watching everything going on around him.

In contrast, John ran all over the pitch and tried to make every tackle count. Why was everyone making such a big thing about Bright, John wondered. What was all the fuss about? Then he found out.

Someone passed the ball to Bright, who yelled, 'Yours, Watt,' and sent the ball sailing half the length of the pitch to land centimetre-perfect at John's feet. John had never seen a pass like it. In a daze, he shuffled goalwards only to feel his legs being taken out from under him. He clattered to the ground with a loud 'Aarghhh!' and rolled around a bit (he'd seen Italian strikers do that on television).

Mr Jones' whistle blew. Free kick! There was a chorus of groans and protests from the defending side and a huge cheer from John's team-mates.

John picked himself up. One or two of his side mouthed 'well done' at him.

As he looked towards the goal, John was surprised to see all of Peters' team lining up in a defensive wall.

Behind them the goalie was gesticulating wildly and shouting instructions. 'Left! More! No, more! Now right! You've got to stop him!'

Bright strode up from the centre circle, picked the ball up and carefully placed it down. Then he looked carefully at where the goal was and where the players were lined up.

The goalie carried on flapping his hands about. 'Left! Too much! Right! Right! Remember it's Bright!'

Surely he's never going to try to score from there, thought John. He's at least twenty-five metres away. Mr Jones blew the whistle. The goalkeeper had his hands clasped in front of him. He seemed to be praying. Bright took three steps backwards, then ran forwards and kicked the ball.

John watched in disbelief as the ball shot past the defensive wall and headed towards the corner flag. Pathetic, he thought, what a . . .

His jaw dropped as the ball seemed to turn at a right angle, and shoot back towards the goal. The goalkeeper made a desperate lunge, but had no chance of stopping the ball as it spun wildly into the top right-hand corner of the goal.

Bright was mobbed by all his team-mates. All except for John who stood gobsmacked. Unbelievable! U-N-BELIEVABLE!

In the changing rooms afterwards, John sat with Bright.

'Unbelievable free kick,' said John. 'That was *unbelievable* what you did – just unbelievable.'

Bright shrugged. 'Not at all. I was simply putting some laws of science into practice. It's all to do with forces; the way you bring your foot into contact with the ball, the angle of delivery, the rotation of the foot, the effect of air resistance . . . all that sort of thing.'

John's brain started to overheat. 'You mean you had to work all that out before you took the kick?'

'Yes,' said Bright matter-of-factly. 'Simple! It's

the same with most ball sports: tennis, baseball, cricket. It's all science!'

'But I hate science,' admitted John.

'You hate science at school,' Bright corrected him. 'Remember though, science isn't just for school. It's for life!'

'That's puppies, isn't it?' asked John, vaguely remembering Christmas adverts from the RSPCA.

'I said science!'

John wasn't totally convinced. 'Right, Bright!'

'One thousand, two hundred and ninety-nine,' snapped Bright. 'I'm counting that one.'

'Sorry.'

Bright picked up his bag. 'Are you doing anything now?'

'No,' answered John.

'In that case, do you fancy coming round to my house for a drink?'

John could hardly speak. Of course he would! His first week and he'd made a friend! A real come-round-to-my-house-for-a-drink-friend! He nodded his head excitedly.

Bright suddenly looked cagey. 'There is a condition though,' he said. 'You've got to sign this.'

He pulled a sheet of yellow paper from his bag and handed it to John. 'Read this, and if you agree to abide by the conditions set down, date it and sign it. Then I'll let you come round.'

John wondered what Bright was going on about. He took the paper and began to read it.

MOST TOP SECRET

CONFIDENTIAL

FOR MY EYES ONLY

I, John Watt, promise that if I visit the home of Vernon Bright Esquire and am invited to share in secret and DANGEROUS confidences, then I will not reveal such aforesaid secret and DANGEROUS confidences to any persons at any time in any place whatsoever.

I also understand that if having signed this document and having been admitted to the home and shared the aforesaid secret and DANGEROUS confidences and I do reveal the aforesaid secret and DANGEROUS confidences to some persons at some place or some time then I will be liable to be

24

```
HURT in various and nasty ways by the
aforementioned Vernon Bright at his
pleasure.
   I swear this, on my life and any other
person's life that matters to me.
   On PAIN OF DEATH.


Signed . . . . . . . . . . . . . . . . . .
Date . . . . . . . . . . . . . . . . . . .
```

John looked up to see if the whole thing was a joke. He'd known Bright for only a week, but the look on his face told John that this was no laughing matter. Bright was serious. Deadly serious.

'Have you read it?' asked Bright.

John nodded. Thank goodness he didn't ask me if I understand it, he thought.

Bright handed John a pen. 'Then sign on the dotted line.'

What's this all about? thought John. Well, if he didn't sign, he'd never find out. He took a deep breath.

And signed.

CHAPTER THREE

The Amazing Banana Trick

'I'll need to call in at Dodgy Dave's on the way home,' Bright said, turning down a side street.

John tried to look as if he understood this remark, and failed. 'What is Dodgy Dave's?' he asked.

Bright led the way through a maze of back alleys, between breakers' yards and small engineering shops. 'Army surplus,' he said briefly.

'You mean, he sells stuff the army . . .'

'Or navy,' said Bright. 'Or air force.'

'Right . . . So he sells stuff they don't need any more . . .?'

Bright shrugged. 'Mostly.'

'Mostly what?'

'Mostly they don't need it any more. Sometimes he gets hold of stuff before they don't need it any more.'

John stared. 'You mean – nicked stuff?'

Bright regarded him with scorn. 'Why do you think he's called Dodgy Dave?' He nodded towards a gateway in a board fence. 'Here we are.'

Dodgy Dave's yard was a jumble of ex- (and almost ex-) military hardware. Stacks of ammunition boxes (practically guaranteed empty) rubbed shoulders with piles of the sort of pots and pans used by cooks who have to provide meals for large numbers of people who aren't fussy about what they eat. In one corner stood a complete armoured car. In another, a pair of lethal-looking missiles poked out from under a camouflage net. They seemed to be threatening a helicopter which had been caught in mid-hover and stuck on a steel pillar, with its rotors anchored by cables as if to stop it escaping.

John stared around, entranced. 'Wow.'

Bright nodded smugly. 'Good, isn't it.' He headed for a door leading into a steel-clad building. The sign above the door said:

DAVID THOMAS VICKERS
Military Surplus Stores
Everything from a Teaspoon
to a Tank!
Come In and Look Around!

John turned from the sign to Bright. 'I thought you said this place was called Dodgy Dave's,' he said accusingly.

Bright rolled his eyes. 'Well, obviously he doesn't call himself that. Be a bit of a giveaway, wouldn't it? That's just what everybody else calls him.' He opened the door. 'Come on.'

Inside, the walls were draped with flags of various nationalities, half-open parachutes and more camouflage nets (including sandy-coloured ones which John supposed were for use in the desert). The rest of the interior was crammed with shelves stacked with all kinds of very-nearly surplus items: uniforms, tents, torches, badges, life jackets, straps, kit bags and tools of all kinds.

John let his breath out in a whoosh. 'It's like an Aladdin's cave.'

Bright looked puzzled. 'No, I think you'll find Aladdin's cave was full of gold and jewels and precious stones and things.' He shook his head dismissively. 'Anyway, this stuff's no good. Junk. Over there's what I need.'

He made a bee line for a dark corner.

This turned out to be full of electronic equipment. There were a few things John recognized: a whole stack of oscilloscopes, a few radar screens, and some tape recorders that looked as if they'd been made for a dinosaur disco. The rest of the stuff was just a collection of gadgets, doo dahs and watchamacallits, piled higgledy-piggledy all over the place.

'Hey, Vernie-baby.'

Bright winced. 'Hello, Dave,' he said without enthusiasm.

Dodgy Dave was a tall, stooping figure with the sort of moustache that shouldn't be allowed. He wore full camouflage gear, an SAS beret and, in spite of his gloomy surroundings, dark sunglasses.

'How y'all doin', Vernie?' he said in a drawl that was supposed to sound Texas, but was closer to Essex.

Bright glared. 'Please don't call me that.' He pulled a scrappy piece of paper out of a pocket and handed it over. 'This is what I need.'

Dave pulled at his moustache as he gazed down the list. 'This I got . . . that I got . . . hoowie!' He let out his breath on a long whistle. 'This ain't even been invented yet! And I ain't seen one of these since I was in 'Nam.' He sighed. 'I'll see what I can do.'

Whistling 'The Star-Spangled Banner', Dodgy Dave disappeared into the inner gloom. The sound of metallic rummaging came out of the darkness.

John tugged Bright's sleeve. 'He said "'Nam". Was he really in Vietnam?'

'No.' Bright was scornful. 'More likely Cheltenham.'

'Oh.' John looked round. 'What are we here for?'

Bright suddenly looked cagey. 'Just to pick up some things.'

'Things?'

'Yes, things. Stuff. This and that.'

'What for?'

Bright eyed his companion narrowly. He seemed to come to a decision.

'For my experiments.'

John was nonplussed. 'Experiments?'

There was a strange light in Bright's eye. 'Haven't you ever wanted to take the world apart to find out what makes it go?'

John regarded him warily. 'No.'

Bright wasn't listening. 'For instance, take magnets.'

John looked around at the piles of equipment. 'Which ones?'

Bright shook his head in annoyance. 'No, I meant . . . Think about magnets.'

'Why?'

'Well, what do you know that's magnetic?'

John had done magnets at his previous school. He frowned. 'Erm – iron and steel really. That's about all.'

'And nickel and cobalt.' Bright looked around, leant closer to John and lowered his voice. 'Ever wondered why other things aren't magnetic?'

John shrugged. 'Such as what?'

Bright looked smug. 'Oh, say . . . a banana.'

John gave him an incredulous look.

Bright pulled something from his pocket and held it out for John's inspection. It was going black, with nasty-looking goo oozing out from cracks in the skin; no self-respecting monkey would even think about eating it, but it was a banana. No doubt about it. John took it from Bright. He weighed it in his hand. He ran his thumb across its surface. He smelt it.

'OK, it's a banana,' he said. 'So?'

Bright gave a sly grin. He pulled one jacket sleeve up. With the air of a conjuror about to pull from his hat, not just a rabbit, but a rabbit playing the banjo, he took the banana. With his other hand, he took a key from his pocket and put it down on a nearby bench.

'Key ... banana,' he said. 'Banana ... key. Observe.'

He held the banana above the key, and slowly lowered it.

When the banana was still several centimetres above it, the key suddenly leapt upwards. John heard a very soft tap.

Bright handed him the banana. The key was stuck to it. John shook it. The key didn't move. He pulled at it. He had to pull quite hard to get it off the banana. He put the key back on the bench, and lowered the banana towards it. This time, John could feel the small impact as the key leapt off the bench and landed on the banana.

John turned incredulous eyes on Bright. Then he grinned sheepishly. 'Oh, I get it,' he said. 'There's a magnet inside, right? What you did, you peeled the banana, and put a steel magnet inside ...' Bright was shaking his head. '... then stuck the peel back ...'

Bright took the banana. 'It's a banana, a whole banana and nothing but a banana.'

'Oh, come ON!'

'Wait until you see my lab.' Bright glared. 'Unless you're not interested, of course ...'

'Oh, I am,' John hastened to reassure him.

Bright grunted and slipped the banana back into his pocket as Dodgy Dave reappeared carrying a plastic tray filled with all sorts of electronic oddments.

'Here y'are,' he drawled. 'I ain't got no phase modulator like you asked for . . .'

Bright sniffed. 'Well, I've got a couple of standard rectifiers. I'll bodge something up.' He took the tray and turned for the door.

Dodgy Dave called after him, 'Hey – you comin' in Saturday?'

'Yes, yes,' said Bright impatiently. 'I know what's wrong with the RDF, and the GPS just needs recalibrating. Make sure you've got the AFCs for the EHF receivers . . .' He swept out in a cloud of jargon. John, feeling that he'd just been listening to a conversation in Martian, hurried to follow.

'I fix things for

him, ' Bright explained as John caught up, 'and he lets me have bits of kit he doesn't need.' He held out the tray. After a moment's hesitation, John took it. 'He doesn't know what half this stuff is, or what it does.' Bright gave a little chuckle. 'Come on then.'

He turned and headed off down the street. John looked down at the tray full of bits. Who did Bright think he was? What gave him the right to just dump trays of stuff on people and expect them to follow him about like some sort of servant or something? I could just drop this tray right here and go home, thought John. He stared at Bright's retreating back. And go to school tomorrow knowing there'd be no one to talk to . . .

With a sigh, he hitched the tray into a more comfortable position, and followed.

The sky had turned steel-grey and threatening by the time they reached Bright's house.

John stood in the road and looked up at it.

'Oh, boy,' he said softly.

Bright's house was a castle.

At least, that's what it looked like. It had fairly normal-looking windows, but it also had a turret in one corner, with a flagpole on top. The pebble-dashed walls were topped with battlements. It looked as if it had been built to withstand a very half-hearted siege.

It was painted pink.

The door was solid wood with iron bands across it. Bright took out the key he had used to demonstrate the magnetic properties of his banana, and pushed it into the lock. He turned it. The door swung open. It should have creaked, but it didn't. Bright stepped inside. After a moment's hesitation, so did John.

Inside, Bright's home was no less weird. John stood in the hall and looked around. The hall was clean enough, and the wallpaper looked new. It took him a few moments to realize what was strange about it.

No two strips of wallpaper were the same.

A pattern of flowers growing through a trellis lay next to one with a green and blue stripe, while a third was decorated with stars and crescent moons. Bright turned and caught John's eye.

'My mother did that,' he said matter-of-factly. 'She says walls are so boring, why make them look the same all the way across? She's an artist,' he went on, as if that explained everything. He went through a doorway.

John found him in the kitchen. Bright was reaching into the fridge – one of the fridges, John realized. There were two. Both had brightly coloured magnetic letters on them. On one, several of the letters had been arranged to spell the word 'fridge'. When Bright closed the door of the other, John saw that some of the letters on it spelt the word 'mortuary'.

'That's part of her cunning plan to turn me and my dad into vegetarians,' said Bright. 'She's a vegan – won't eat anything from a fridge that's had meat in it. My dad's away at the moment. Actually, he's away most of the time. Coke?'

John nodded. 'Where is your mum?'

'She'll be up in her studio, painting,' said Bright. 'The roof's mostly glass, for the light. She has the top of the house, I have the bottom. We sort of meet in the middle. Sometimes.'

Carrying two cans of Coke in one hand, Bright moved to a corner of the room and pulled aside a curtain. Behind the curtain was a door.

Instead of opening it, Bright reached towards a keypad set into the wall beside the door jamb. He tapped in a sequence of numbers too quickly for John to follow, then pressed the palm of his free hand against a flat black plate above the keypad. The plate glowed briefly and a red light appeared on the keypad display.

Bright stepped aside. 'Security system,' he said. 'It'll need to record your palm print. Put your hand on the plate.'

Feeling a bit of a fool, and balancing the tray of bits on one hand, John did so. The pad glowed again and he felt a vague tingling sensation.

Bright then put his eye to a peephole set in the middle of the door. Funny, John thought, peepholes are supposed to be for people on the inside seeing who is on the outside.

A green light appeared on the keypad. Bright gestured John to follow his lead. 'Retina scan,' he said briefly.

John stared at him.

'Can't be too careful.'

John swallowed. 'So this would be a bit of nearly ex-gear from the secret services, would it? Something from MI5?'

'MI6.'

John nodded wordlessly and put his eye to the peephole. There was a tiny flash.

'Now the security system will let me know it's you if I'm inside and you come round,' explained Bright. He tapped another sequence of numbers into the pad. The door gave a click and swung slightly ajar.

Bright stood aside and gestured John to go through. 'Welcome to my lab.'

CHAPTER FOUR

Animal Magnetism

'Of course, most of this stuff belongs to my dad,' explained Bright airily as he walked down the stone steps into the basement. 'He doesn't mind me using it while he's away.' He flicked a switch; the cellar flooded with light.

The Bright basement was a genuine state-of-the-art and all-mod-cons-included Mad Scientist's laboratory. In the centre of the lab stood a large machine with its insides hanging out. It had a satellite dish, or a baby radio telescope on top of it. All round the room, half-finished (or abandoned) machines bristled with buttons, switches, screens, and unidentifiable bits of electronic gadgetry. There were tanks round the wall that bubbled – John really, really hoped they were empty – and nasty things floated in jars.

There was even a stuffed crocodile hanging from the ceiling (most kids are happy with model aeroplanes, John thought) with a pained expression on its face and 'A Present from Daar Es Salaam' written on its side.

John cleared his throat. 'What does your dad actually do?' he asked.

Bright put the Cokes down and held a hand out for the tray of bits. 'He works for the government. You know sometimes scientists do things that come within a split second of causing nuclear devastation or destroying the world?'

John Watt nodded enthusiastically. 'Yes, like in films. Satellites with laser death rays that go loopy and try to destroy London, stuff like that. Your dad stops things like that happening, does he?'

Bright looked uncomfortable. 'Well, no, usually he's the one making them happen. Not on purpose, of course,' he went on hastily, 'but there are always bound to be risks at the cutting edge of new technologies.'

'Right . . .' said John slowly.

'Anyway, he hasn't destroyed the world yet. I

mean, we're still here, aren't we? Have a Coke.'

As John sipped from the can, Bright bustled about switching equipment on. Then he sat at a workbench and rummaged through the bits they'd collected from Dodgy Dave's. He selected a couple of gizmos, and some electric wires from a plastic tub. He started to fit the new bits into something that looked like an exploded radio.

'Hold this, will you?' Bright passed John a coil of solder while he checked the temperature of a soldering iron on a sponge pad. Evidently satisfied, he took the solder back and started to connect a piece of wire to a dull grey implement that looked like a cross between a potato masher and a hand grenade.

'So how do you magnetize a banana?' John took another sip from his can.

'Actually, I think lots of things can be magnetized. It's just that nobody knows how to do it . . .' Bright looked smug. 'Except me.'

'Such as what?'

Bright clicked his tongue irritably. 'What do you want, a list?'

'Well, have you made anything else magnetic? Apart from the banana?'

Bright waved towards a shelf. 'Take a look in that glass jar.'

John reached up to the shelf and took down a glass jar. He looked inside.

The jar was half-full of what looked like leaf-mould. Something moved in the depths. As John gazed, a humped shape broke the surface, and uncoiled. Something long and furry waved about

bonelessly for a moment or two before subsiding back into the dirt.

'I can't see it properly,' John complained. 'Something waved about – it could have been a hairy leg. Have you got a tarantula in there?'

Bright smirked. 'No.'

'Well, then, it must be one of those big hairy caterpillars,' John said uncertainly.

Bright gave him a twisted grin. 'Not even close.'

John was getting exasperated. 'A tentacle off a very small, hairy octopus?' he said sarcastically.

'Now you're just being silly.'

'Well, what is it then?'

'It's a worm.'

'A hairy worm?' John gave Bright a look of pure disbelief.

'A magnetic worm. The "hairs" are iron filings.' Bright pushed the soldering iron into its holster. 'Look.' He took a silver and red bar magnet from a drawer and laid it on the workbench. Then he pulled a blank sheet of paper from a wire tray, and gave it to John. He took the top off a jar half-filled with black powder, and shook about a tablespoonful on to the paper.

'Now,' he said, 'lower the paper slowly over the magnet.'

As John lowered the paper, Bright tapped gently on one side. The powder started to form curved lines around each end of the magnet beneath.

'Those are called flux lines. The iron filings settle along the lines of force being produced by the magnet.' Bright reached under the paper and held up the magnet. 'Of course, if the paper wasn't there, the iron filings would just stick to the magnet. Like they have to the worm.' He stroked the paper with one end of the magnet. The black powder immediately stuck to the magnet, making it look as if it had a hairy end.

John looked at the magnet. He looked into the jar.

The front end of the worm (John assumed it was the front end) pushed up out of the dirt again. It waved its hairy snout about in a forlorn sort of way.

'Does the worm like being covered with iron filings?' John asked.

Bright raised his eyebrows. 'I don't know. It hasn't said.'

'Isn't that a bit cruel?'

'Is it?' Bright shrugged.

'Can't you get the filings off it?'

'Ah, well . . .' Bright looked sheepish. 'I haven't worked out how to do that bit yet. I can make things magnetic – at least, anything with traces of iron in it – but once a thing's magnetized, I haven't found a way to de-magnetize it.'

John said nothing, but he couldn't help feeling that this was rather rough luck for the worm.

Bright picked up more wires, a digital alarm clock and a computer circuit board and went back to his soldering. He held the solder between his teeth, which made his voice rather muffled. 'You fee, all akoms have magnefic properties . . .'

'All akoms?'

'I *fed* . . .' Bright sighed and took the solder out of his mouth. 'I *said*, all atoms have magnetic properties, but some atoms are much more magnetic than others. Why don't you listen?' He put the soldering iron down again. 'Look; take this nail,' he picked one up off the desk, 'and try and pick up that paperclip.'

John poked the nail at a paperclip lying on the worktop. It completely failed to respond in any way.

'I can't,' he said.

Bright nodded. 'That's because the nail is made of iron, but it hasn't been magnetized.' He took another bar magnet from the bench drawer and tossed it to John. 'Now stroke the nail across the magnet.'

Bright placed a set of bathroom scales next to the strange-looking contraption he was assembling and made another solder connection as John stroked the nail. Bright grunted with satisfaction and turned back to John. 'OK, now touch the nail on to that paperclip.'

John did so. The clip stuck to the nail. John lifted it off the workbench, and watched it swing about.

'You see,' Bright said, 'in the nail, the magnetic forces of the atoms are clumped together into groups called domains. These domains are very small – less than a millimetre across normally.'

John's brow furrowed with concentration. 'Yeeesssss . . .' he said slowly.

'Domains are like tiny magnets,' Bright went on. 'Before you stroked the nail with the magnet, all its domains were jumbled up, so all the magnetic forces were working in different directions. But when you stroked the magnet against it, you made the domains in the nail line up in the same direction. Its magnetic forces started working together instead of against each other, and the nail became a magnet. Of course, that way you can only magnetize stuff that's attracted by magnets anyway.'

'Why?'

'Because in metals like iron and steel, the domains line up very easily.'

The paperclip fell off the end of the nail and bounced off the workbench and on to the floor.

'But with iron, they don't stay lined up for very long, so the nail loses its magnetism again. Steel takes longer to magnetize, but it keeps its magnetism for longer. Other stuff doesn't magnetize at all.' Bright's eyes glinted. 'But why not? Lots of things contain iron, so why can't anything that has iron in it be made magnetic?'

John tapped the nail on the edge of the workbench. 'So you decided to see if you could make other stuff magnetic.'

'Yes. And I did it! I've created a force field that can line up the magnetic forces in iron, even if it's traces of iron in an animal, or a fruit . . .'

'Like the banana.'

'And the worm. But I need more power to try it out on something bigger. That's why I needed the stuff from Dave's.' Bright started soldering again. 'I'm building a new amplifier for the force field, and then . . .' he gave a grin that made John move back a step '. . . I'll be ready to try it out on a guinea pig.'

John felt himself go cold all over. Surely Bright hadn't pretended to be friendly and lured him here to use him in some loony experiment?

'A g-g-guinea pig?' he stammered.

'Oh, yes,' Bright said softly. He leered at John, who felt himself go cold with dread. Bright was mad. He was going to whip out a handkerchief soaked in chloroform in a minute – or perhaps he'd put something in the Coke? John pushed his can away in horror, and began to edge towards the door.

'I knew that I would need to try out my magnetic generator on some insignificant, worthless creature,' said Bright. 'A lower form of life.'

'Hey, steady on!' John was offended, in spite of his terror.

Bright picked up something that looked like a death-ray gun and came towards John. 'Now for the moment of truth.'

John looked desperately around for some sort of weapon. His hand closed over something smooth and curved. His finger circled around its trigger. He pointed it at Bright.

'Do you see what I've got here?' he shrieked.

'Yes,' said Bright. 'It's a plant spray.'

'That's right! And I'm not afraid to use it!'

Bright put his head on one side and regarded John quizzically. 'What are you going on about?'

'You said you were going to try your machine out on a guinea pig!'

'Yes.' Bright jerked his head. 'He's in that cage over there. His name's Horace.'

John peered into the cage. There was a guinea pig inside. It stared woodenly back at him and chewed a bit of carrot.

'Oh.' John felt very foolish. 'What's that thing you're carrying?'

Bright looked at the 'ray gun' in his hands. 'It's a particle accelerator. Part of the magnetic force generator. I'm just going to install it.' He opened a hatch in the side of the machine with the baby satellite dish and slotted it in.

John gave a cough of embarrassment. 'Erm – you know when people say they're going to do experiments on a guinea pig? I think it's just an expression. I don't think it means you have to use an actual guinea pig.'

Bright stared at him. 'Really? I didn't know that.' He shook his head, dismissing the matter. 'Well, anyway, I'm ready.' He picked up the gadget he had been working on, carried it over to the machine, and started to connect wires. 'Could you get Horace out for me?'

John's terror had evaporated, to be replaced by anger. 'No, I won't,' he said.

'It's all right.' Bright looked up. 'He doesn't bite.'

'That's not the point.' John had had about enough of Bright and his superior manner and his covering worms with itchy black dust. 'What gives you the right to do your stupid experiments on some poor animal that can't defend itself?'

Bright was moving the thing that looked like a radio telescope so that the dish was pointing at the top of a table. He gave John a scornful look. 'It's a lot more sensible than doing experiments on an animal that *can* defend itself. Anyway, I'm not going to hurt it.'

'How do you know? You might fry it to a crisp. Even if you don't, you'll scare it half to death pointing that thing at it!'

Bright regarded him coldly. 'If you're not going to help, just keep out of the way.' He went over to the cage and took the guinea pig out. Horace carried on nibbling his carrot and eyed him stolidly. Bright carried the guinea pig over and put it in the centre of the table.

John bit his lip as Bright went round to the back

of the machine. Unaware of the danger he was in, Horace sat and chewed as Bright flicked switches and tapped a sequence of commands into the computer controlling the machine. A low hum came from the dish and started to build in pitch. Bright reached into his pocket and pulled out a pair of tinted goggles, which he put on. The machine's hum built to a whine. John stared helplessly at the defenceless guinea pig.

'Just a few more seconds,' said Bright.

John darted forward. His one thought was to grab Horace before Bright managed to roast the unfortunate rodent, but as he reached out, his arm caught the dish of the machine. The dish swung round until it was pointing straight at Bright.

There was an explosion of sound and a sudden, brilliant flash . . .

Then silence. The lights on the machine went out.

John sat on the floor, cradling Horace in his hands. Bright stood stock still, apparently in shock. He removed his goggles with one trembling hand. With the other, he pointed a quivering finger at John.

'What have you done?' he whispered.

Something small and bright leapt off the floor, towards Bright's outstretched arm.

Both Bright and John stared in horrified fascination. A paper clip had stuck firmly to Bright's pointing finger.

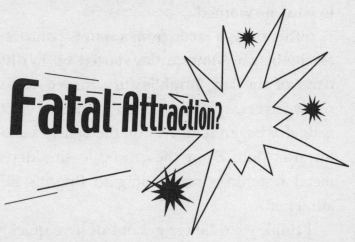

CHAPTER FIVE

Fatal Attraction?

'You're a magnet!' John cried out.

'And whose stupid fault is that!' snapped Bright.

'It's your fault!' said John defensively. 'You shouldn't have tried to experiment on Horace.' The guinea pig chewed on, oblivious to its lucky escape. John put it back in its cage.

'My fault?' howled Bright incredulously. 'Who moved the dish? Not me! And Horace wouldn't have minded,' he went on, with less conviction.

Several more paper clips jumped through the air towards Bright. One landed right on the tip of his nose. Bright glared as a grin spread over John's face. 'And if you make any jokes about me having a magnetic personality, I will do something terrible to you,' he warned.

There was a rattle from a set of spanners lying on the bench. More rattles started up in different parts of the lab. Bright's fury turned to fear as screwdrivers, spanners and all kinds of electronic gadgetry began to quiver on the benches and turn towards him. Even the crocodile shuddered, its metal fastenings responding to Bright's field of attraction.

'I think we'd better get out of here quickly,' he said, backing away. The tools continued to twitch as if sensing the newly created magnet.

John's amusement was turning to alarm. 'What's going on?' he asked.

'I think my magnetic force is growing,' groaned Bright. Every metal object in the laboratory began to shake uncontrollably. Even Horace's cage started to shake. It seemed as though the whole lab was coming alive.

'GET OUT!' yelled Bright, heading towards the lab door.

John didn't need telling twice; he raced after Bright. The two boys pounded up the stairs as the rattling grew to a crescendo. Bright paused for a micro-second in order to hit a button on the wall that said 'EMERGENCY'. The lab door flew open just as several spanners began to fly through the air.

They got out just in time. Bright slammed the door behind him and stood with his back against it, arms held out wide. Behind him, there was an almighty crash as the metallic contents of the lab flung themselves against the door. John flinched as he heard a high-pitched *'Squuuueakkkkkkkk!'* that seemed to be the sound a guinea pig might make if it was flying through the air. Poor Horace; I hope he's all right, John thought.

He turned towards the kitchen door. 'Let's get out of here,' he said.

'Help,' said Bright plaintively.

John turned. Bright hadn't moved from his position. He was still plastered to the lab door.

John sighed in exasperation. 'The door's closed. You can come away from it.'

'I can't.' Bright struggled feebly. 'This door's made of steel. I'm stuck to it.'

John raised his eyes to heaven. He went back to Bright, grabbed his arms, and started to pull. And pull. And pull . . .

Bright suddenly shot forward as the magnetic grip of the door was broken. From behind it came the crash and clatter of lab equipment falling to the floor and bouncing down the stone steps into the cellar.

Bright staggered into the kitchen, and was immediately enveloped in a shower of magnetic letters. John ducked and wildly flapped his arms as the letters flew off the fridge doors like a horde of locusts.

John turned and looked at Bright. The letters had stuck to his body. He gave the appearance of someone who had stood next to an exploding can of alphabet spaghetti.

John burst out laughing. The letters N, E, R and D were stuck on Bright's forehead.

'What's so funny?' scowled Bright.

'The letters on your forehead spell . . .' John saw Bright looking daggers at him. 'They spell . . . oh, it doesn't matter. I suppose it's not that funny.'

'No. It isn't,' Bright assured him and backed away from the fridge doors.

As Bright moved, he sensed something was following him. He turned quickly. There was a portable radio on the fridge. Its aerial was pointing straight at him. Bright took a pace to his left. The aerial followed him. He took another step. The aerial mirrored the movement.

An awful thought suddenly struck Bright. He glanced at the kitchen work tops and gave a muffled 'oh no!'. Every single electrical item in the kitchen was quivering as they felt the attraction of Bright's altered state.

'John ... do something!' ordered Bright through clenched teeth. 'I think I'm going to be ... AARRGGHHHHH!' Bright screamed as the air became a blur of flying objects.

John flung himself to the floor and scrunched shut his eyes, not wanting to see his new-found friend battered into a pulp.

After a second or two, the rush of air stopped and there was silence. John slowly opened his eyes and looked up, afraid of what he was going to see.

It wasn't what he'd expected.

Bright stood shaking in the middle of the kitchen. He was surrounded by a variety of electrical items which were hovering in mid air. They were all held back from Bright by their cords, which were still fixed to the wall plugs. John took a quick inventory: kettle, toaster, coffee grinder, food processor, microwave, juicer, radio and several other items of a 'cupboard-under-the-sink' variety, whose purpose wasn't exactly clear. They looked like a pack of fierce dogs on leashes, all straining in a desperate attempt to attach themselves to Bright's body.

Bright stood in the middle of the hovering mass, hardly daring to breathe. He turned to his left to see the microwave hovering a couple of centimetres from his nose.

Bright gulped. 'Now I want you to listen to me very carefully,' he told John. 'I want you to clear my path to the door. The way you do this is, you unplug the things that are between me and the door. I want you to unplug them one by one, very, very carefully, and take them through into the next room. Make sure you keep hold of the leads. Are you ready?'

John nodded. He crept up on the microwave, which was twitching on the end of its power lead. 'I think this oven has got the hots for you,' he quipped.

Bright glared at him. 'Spare me your idiotic comments, please,' he hissed. 'Just get rid of it!'

After John had wrestled the microwave into submission, he subdued the juicer. The electric kettle put up a terrific fight, but the toaster went relatively quietly. Then John approached an electric carving knife with some trepidation.

'This thing looks sharp,' he said. 'Has it got a guard or something?'

'In that cupboard over there, with the cutlery,' said Bright automatically, backing towards the door while keeping his eyes fixed on the coffee grinder which was making a particularly spirited attempt to clobber him between the eyes.

John moved over to a large cupboard and grabbed hold of the door handle. 'What, this one?'

Bright had reached the door. His eyes bulged as he realized what was about to happen. 'NOOOOOOOOOOOO!' he wailed.

He was too late. John had yanked the cupboard door open. A swarm of spoons, forks and knives flew out. It was as if a circus knife thrower had gone crazy. Bright's head jerked from side to side as knives scythed passed him and embedded themselves in the door. He ducked just in time as a meat-cleaver, whirling end-over-end, sliced into the wood just above his head, parting his hair neatly down the middle.

The swarm of cutlery was followed by a flock of pans and other kitchen utensils. Try as he might, Bright couldn't avoid the barrage of cookware and his howls mingled with the clatter of kitchen implements attaching themselves forcefully to him.

'Ow! Eek! Oooh! Aargh! Help! Oooohoo-hoohooooooooooo!'

Within seconds the mayhem had died down. The electrical goods shivered in sympathy with Bright.

John regarded his friend with interest. He was covered in cooking utensils: spoons, forks, spatulas, several pans and their lids, a potato peeler, apple corer, several whisks, three corkscrews, a wok and a pair of nut crackers hung from various parts of Bright's body. He looked like a huge metal porcupine.

The 'porcupine' spoke. 'Now, I want you to listen to me even more carefully than last time. I want you to get this stuff off me, one piece at a time. Don't open any more drawers or cupboards. And for starters,' he added, 'you can get this cheese grater off my nose. But don't drag it!'

CHAPTER SIX

A Striking Development

'What am I going to do?' wailed Bright.

He sat quivering on a cushion in the exact centre of the sitting room, from which John had carefully removed everything made of metal (except the TV set which, though it had steel components, was too big to move and sat in a corner twitching occasionally).

John shrugged. 'Will it wear off?' he asked.

'I doubt it. I magnetized the worm a week ago, and it's still magnetic.'

'Well, you'll just have to stay away from metal objects.'

Bright gave him a furious look. 'Oh, yes, that'll be dead easy, won't it? I can't go in the kitchen.

Can't use a knife and fork. How do I get to school on Monday? If I get on the bus, I'll never get off it! I can't go in a car.' Bright's voice rose in a crescendo of misery. 'Can't go up an escalator; can't get in a lift; can't play the guitar . . .'

'I didn't know you played the guitar,' said John with interest.

'I don't, but I couldn't now even if I wanted to, that's the *point*,' snapped Bright irritably.

'Ah, no, you couldn't play a steel-string guitar,' said John, 'but you could play the Spanish guitar, because that hasn't got steel strings. Or a violin. And you could play the recorder. But you couldn't play the saxophone, or . . .'

'Will you stop blathering!' roared Bright. 'Just shut up about musical instruments, all right?'

'Well, you were the one who . . .'

'*All right?*'

John subsided. There was an awkward pause before Bright started moaning again. 'The worst of it is, I can't even try to find out how to stop myself being magnetic. I daren't go into the lab, I can't use metal tools, and any instruments I try to use will probably beat me to death!'

'Maybe I can help,' suggested John.

Bright gave him a withering look. 'I doubt it.'

John was nettled. 'Well, I know I'm not a scientific genius like you,' he said. 'Of course, not being a scientific genius, *I've* never been intelligent enough to turn myself into a living magnet, so of course I wouldn't know how to help you. In fact, I think I'd better go . . .' He headed for the door.

'No!' Bright leapt to his feet. The TV quivered

threateningly and Bright sat down again hurriedly. 'I . . . I . . . I'm sorry.' He seemed to have difficulty getting the words out; John realized that Bright probably wasn't used to apologizing, or asking for help. It wasn't so much that he was unwilling – he simply wasn't sure how you did it. Now he was looking at the carpet and wringing his hands.

'I didn't mean . . . when I said . . .' He turned an anguished face to John. 'Help me . . . please?'

John retraced his steps and sat down on the sofa. 'OK. Look, let's start at the beginning. Maybe we'll think of something that way. That machine of yours turned you into a magnet, I understand that much, but I don't understand how it did it.'

Bright brushed his fingers through his hair. 'Well, that's a bit complicated. How can I explain?' He thought for a moment. Then he said, 'Pass me the box of matches on the mantelpiece.'

When John had done this, Bright went on, 'Remember in the lab, when I showed you how to magnetize the nail?' John nodded.

Bright opened the matchbox and tilted it so that John could see the matches lying neatly in rows. 'In a magnet, all the magnetic fields are lined up in the same direction, like the matches in here.'

He tipped the box upside down and the matches fell on to the carpet. They lay in an untidy, spiky heap. 'But in any non-magnetic object,' Bright said, 'the magnetic fields are all jumbled up like this; so the magnetic effects cancel each other out.'

John scratched his head. 'But I still don't see . . .'

Bright interrupted him. 'Remember how you made the nail magnetic by stroking it against the magnet? What you were doing was making the magnetic fields line up. But an ordinary magnet can only do that to magnetic materials like iron and steel.'

'Where the magnetic fields are already grouped in dom . . . domdoodahs.'

'Domains. That's right. What my machine does is to line up the magnetic fields of iron atoms in anything that contains even a trace of iron. Somehow – I haven't worked out exactly how yet – it also boosts their magnetic effect. Bananas contain iron. So do worms.' He looked sheepish. 'So do I.'

'So, what you're saying,' said John slowly, 'is that all the iron atoms in your body have magnetic fields, and all their fields have been lined up the same way. But if lining the fields up makes you magnetic, then all we have to do to make you un-magnetic is to jumble the fields up again.'

'Oh, yes,' said Bright bitterly, 'that's *all*.'

'Well, isn't there any way of doing that?' asked John.

Bright thought deeply. 'There are only two ways that I know of. A magnetic object can lose its magnetism *if*,' he raised two fingers and ticked the ways off, 'one – it is heated to a high temperature. Two – it is struck a sharp blow.'

John raised his eyebrows. 'As simple as that?'

'Yes. Raising the temperature causes the atoms to move about, so the domains naturally fall out of line with each other, and a sharp blow just knocks the domains out of kilter. Either way, the magnetism should disappear. It works on bar magnets, I know, I've done it, but you have to hit them pretty hard.'

John nodded to himself. 'Just a minute.' He went out of the room. A series of clanks and clatters sounded from the hallway as he rummaged in the cupboard under the stairs.

Left to himself, Bright began to wallow in his own misery. 'Why do these things always happen to me? Whenever I try to push back the boundaries of knowledge, something goes wrong and . . .'

'Will this do?'

Bright turned round slowly. John was standing in the doorway. He was holding a cricket bat.

Bright stared at him. 'Do for what?'

John waved the cricket bat. 'For hitting you over the head with?'

'Sorry?'

'You know – to de-magnetize you.'

'You're not hitting me over the head with that!'

John's face fell. 'Oh, go on. It won't hurt.'

'Yes it will!' howled Bright.

'You're right, it will. I was just trying to reassure you.'

'Don't even think about it!'

John said in a hurt voice, 'I thought it would help you get rid of your magnetism. You said a sharp blow would do it.'

'*Might* do it. *Might!* I've no idea how hard you'd have to hit me to make any difference.'

'I'll hit you as hard as I can . . .' John promised.

'Oh, thank you very much!' yelled Bright. 'You're loving this, aren't you? You've been wanting to hit me ever since you met me,

70

everybody does, and now you've got the perfect excuse, haven't you? What have I done to deserve this? I only wanted to see if I could make living things magnetic, and now I'm stuck here with . . . *Where do you think you're going?!'*

John held up the cricket bat. 'Well, I thought I'd put this away if you don't want it.' His face brightened. 'I can try and find something heavier if you like. Have you got a sledgehammer?'

Bright stared at him, speechless.

John warmed to his topic. 'Just think, one good thump from a sledgehammer would solve all your problems . . .'

'Oh, it would do that all right,' Bright snarled sarcastically. 'It would solve all my problems by *crushing my skull like an eggshell, did you ever think of that*?!'

John looked crestfallen. 'I'm only trying to help.'

'Don't try to help me! Just sit still over there, where I can see you, while I try to think of something, OK?'

John sighed. 'OK.'

Bright sat on his cushion, lost in thought. After an awkward silence, John asked, 'Mind if I put the TV on?'

'Go ahead.'

John switched the set on and reached for the remote control. A harsh crackle came from the speakers. The screen filled with an interference pattern. John frowned and jabbed buttons. On every channel it was the same. No picture, no sound, just interference. He called to Bright, 'Hey – is this thing working?'

'It was last night.' Bright looked up briefly. 'Maybe it's a transmission fault.'

'Not on all channels.'

Bright stood up very, very carefully. 'All this talk about hitting me with sledgehammers is giving me a headache. I'm going to the bathroom for some painkillers.'

John nodded and continued to press buttons. As soon as Bright left the room, a channel flashed up on the screen, bright and clear.

'Oh – it's OK,' John called. There was a clatter from the bathroom. 'The picture's back.'

Bright came back into the room. He had a towel-holder stuck to his upper lip. He looked like a bull with an oversized nose-ring.

Instantly, the TV picture went fuzzy again.

Bright pulled the ring away from his mouth and

held it out to John, who took it. Wordlessly, he left the room again.

'Picture's back,' John reported.

Bright came back in.

'Gone again,' said John, as the screen fizzled. He looked across at Bright. 'It's you doing it, isn't it?'

Bright groaned. 'I must be generating some kind of electromagnetic interference. I can't even watch TV any more!'

A few minutes' cautious experimentation revealed that Bright's presence also affected radios, which howled; the computer in his dad's study, which started to calculate the value of pi in Roman numerals; and the Bright family cat, which arched its back and spat at him.

Back in the sitting room, Bright sat on his cushion rocking backwards and forwards, moaning softly in despair. 'How am I going to solve this mess when I can't even use a computer?'

John clicked his fingers. 'Wait a minute. What was the other thing you said could destroy magnetism?'

'Heat can, but . . .'

'I've got an idea.'

*

73

Bright sat on his bed. He was wearing two balaclavas, three thick pullovers, three pairs of jogging-bottoms and two coats. He had an electric blanket and a duvet wrapped round his shoulders, open at the front where a fan heater was blowing full-blast. Hot-water bottles nestled around him. Sweat poured down his face. He was feverishly leafing through a pile of scientific textbooks.

John came in carrying a fresh hot-water bottle. Wordlessly, Bright pulled a hottie from inside his pullovers, handed it to John, and replaced it with the fresh one. He carried on leafing.

'I'm sure this isn't going to work,' he moaned.

John shrugged and sat on the bed. 'Have you got any better ideas?'

Bright scowled and said nothing.

'Should I turn the central heating up a bit more?'

Suddenly, Bright gave a howl of despair. He pointed a shaking finger at a paragraph in the book.

'Here it is! Temperature at which iron loses its magnetism – seven hundred and sixty degrees Celsius!' He snatched the balaclavas from his head and dashed them to the floor. He started to struggle out of the blanket-and-duvet cocoon, muttering savagely.

'Don't you think we could get you that hot?' asked John innocently.

Bright paused and regarded him scornfully. 'Water boils at one hundred degrees Celsius. Chips fry at two hundred degrees. If you want to find out what seven hundred and sixty degrees feels like, try sticking your finger on the bar of an electric fire! No, I do not think we can get my body heat up to seven hundred and sixty degrees Celsius.' He wriggled out of another layer.

John sighed and picked up the book Bright had been reading. He turned it over and looked at the cover. Bright had just dragged the last pullover over his head, breathing heavily, when John clicked his fingers.

'The bloke who wrote this book,' he said. 'Professor B. G. Brayn . . .'

Bright stared at John. 'Well? What about him?'

'Well, it says here he's the world's leading expert on fer . . . ro . . . magn . . .' John squinted in an attempt to read the unfamiliar word.

'Ferromagnetism, I know.' Bright ran his fingers through his damp hair. 'He does experiments on magnetic fields in living things. So?'

'Could he help?'

Bright stuck his chin out and looked mulish. 'How? If he knew as much about magnetizing living things as I do, he'd have worked out how to do it before I did!'

'Maybe, but at least he can do experiments without having all the lab equipment attack him. Anyway, it says on the back of the book that he works at the Natural History Museum. In London. We could go tomorrow. My mum's out all day, she won't miss me.' He looked at Bright expectantly.

Bright gave him an incredulous look. 'You want to drag me to London? Are you crazy? I can sort this out by myself!'

He stalked out of the room. There was a clatter from the landing.

John leant against the door frame and watched Bright battling with the hose of the vacuum cleaner, which was wrapped round him like the tentacles of a giant squid.

'Wanna bet?' he said.

John followed Bright into the hall. 'I'll call round at nine o'clock, OK?' Keeping his eyes on the back of Bright's head, he reached towards the hall table.

As Bright reached for the front door-handle to open it for his guest, something smashed over his head. Water drenched his hair and trickled down the back of his neck. Some slightly wilted flowers flopped over his shoulders. Bits of crockery fell to the floor.

Bright turned round incredulously. He stared at John, who was holding the remains of a flower vase in his hands and gazing at him expectantly.

As Bright blinked water from his shocked eyes, John took a paper clip out of his pocket and held it out. He let it go. It flew straight to Bright and stuck on his ear.

John shrugged. He gave the thunderstruck Bright a cheerful grin.

'Worth a try.'

CHAPTER SEVEN

Rough Ride

'This is ridiculous,' Bright protested. 'I don't need any help.'

'Yeah. Right.' John was getting breathless. The road to the station was lined with old-fashioned cast-iron lamp-posts. John had had to drag Bright away from every single one of them: seventeen so far.

And a pillar box.

'You're worse than my gran's corgi. That won't leave lamp-posts alone either.' John gave an almighty tug and Bright came free.

Bright gave him an unfriendly look. 'When I say I don't need help, I mean obviously I need help from you at the moment to pull me off things. But

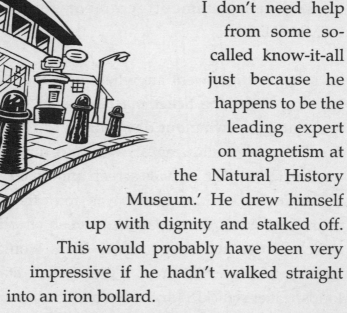

I don't need help from some so-called know-it-all just because he happens to be the leading expert on magnetism at the Natural History Museum.' He drew himself up with dignity and stalked off. This would probably have been very impressive if he hadn't walked straight into an iron bollard.

'Heeelllllllppppp meeeeeeeeee,' he squeaked as soon as he could squeak anything. 'I'mmmm stuuuuuck.'

'Only your bottom half,' said John unsympathetically.

Snarling with rage, Bright leant forward to make a grab at John – and folded over the bollard like a book snapping shut. He lay draped over it with his nose stuck to one side and his ankles to the other.

John bent down and said sweetly, 'My gran's corgi really likes that bollard. It's one of his particular favourites.'

'Gemmeoffgemmeoffgemmeoffgemmeoff-
GEMMEOFF!'

As soon as Bright went anywhere near the station
booking office, the ticket machine went haywire
and started spewing out day returns to Hastings.
The TV screens showing arrivals and departures
went mad too. The arrivals screen announced that
the train from Birmingham was four thousand
years late, while the departures screen cheerfully
indicated that the next train to Mars would be
leaving from Platform Five. The station
loudspeakers crackled and the platform announce-
ments were replaced by the News in Welsh.

John bought tickets and they headed for the
platform. Several people stared at them.

'I told you not to wear sunglasses,' Bright hissed
out of the corner of his mouth. 'You're making us
look conspicuous.'

John pulled the glasses down his nose and
stared at Bright over the frames. 'Have you looked
in a mirror lately?'

'No, why?'

'Your jacket's ripped where I pulled you away
from the bollard, you've got a dozen drinks cans

sticking to you from when we walked past that wastebin, and you've got a baggage trolley stuck to your bottom. It waggles when you walk.'

Bright tried to push the trolley away in disgust. It stuck to his hand. 'I wondered what was making all the noise. How on earth did that get there?'

John pushed the trolley out of range. 'I don't know, but I know what's making us look conspicuous and it isn't my sunglasses.'

As soon as they reached the steps going down to the platform, Bright staggered, then sank to his knees. John stared at him. 'Those should be all right – they're concrete or something, aren't they?'

Bright raised an anguished face. 'Must be a ... steel frame ... underneath ... pulling me down ...'

Even with John's best efforts to support him, Bright could only crawl down the steps to the platform. Two elderly lady passengers going up the steps eyed him with disgust. One whispered something to the other.

John caught the words. He giggled. 'They think you've been drinking.'

The London train was waiting at the platform.

At the bottom of the steps, Bright shook John off ungratefully. 'All right. The platform is concrete, so there shouldn't be any more problems. Let's just get on the train, and try not to make any more of a spectacle of ourselves . . .'

'Ha!' John turned on his heel and walked towards the carriages. 'What do you mean, "ourselves?"' he asked crossly. 'It's you who . . .'

He realized that he was talking to himself, and turned.

Bright was standing close to the engine. Very close.

In fact he had his nose, and much of the rest of him, pressed right up against it.

John raised his eyes to heaven, and strolled back towards him. 'And the record for the world's most short-sighted train-spotter goes to . . .'

The panic in Bright's voice was unmistakable. 'I'm not looking at the engine, you stupid idiot. I'm stuck to it!'

John gazed at him in alarm. 'Come on, stop mucking about, the train'll start going in a minute.'

'I KNOW THAT! Pull me off it!'

John tugged with all his might. For a moment, he thought he had succeeded, but all that happened

was that he pulled the sleeve off Bright's jacket and turned him over so that he was stuck, spreadeagled, with his back to the engine instead of his front.

Bright stared at John with bloodshot eyes. 'There must be masses of iron and steel inside here. Dirty huge great engines, accumulators, transformers, all sorts of gear, tons and tons of it. You'll never pull me off it!'

John bit his knuckles. 'What am I going to do?'

Bright grinned madly at him. 'Well, I know what I'm going to do.'

'Yes? What?'

Bright drew in a deep lungful of air, and yelled at the top of his voice, 'I'm going to *die* while you're dithering around! Find a way to stop this train!'

John sped off down the platform. He screeched to a halt beside a man holding a whistle and something that looked like an outsized lollipop.

'Excuse me,' he said, 'you've got to stop this train.'

The man stared at him. 'Is that right?' he said. 'Why?'

'My friend's on it.'

The man stared at him some more. 'Well, if he's going to London, he's in the right place, and if he isn't, he'd better get off quick because this train is leaving.' He raised the whistle to his lips.

John was frantic. 'No, you don't understand. He's stuck on it.'

The man shook his head. 'He can't be. The doors don't lock till the train starts to move.'

John screeched in frustration, 'He's not stuck ON it, he's stuck TO it!'

The man glared at him. 'Very funny, son.' He didn't look at the front of the train. He blew his whistle. He waved his lollipop.

John made a dash for the nearest door. He

yanked it open just moments before the train began to move. He dived through it and dragged it shut behind him.

The railway official was running along the platform, tapping on the glass. John pulled the window down. 'What?'

"Ere, have you got a ticket?'

For a moment, John stared him in the face. Then his carriage passed the end of the platform and the railway official dropped suddenly from view. Looking back along the train, John could see him sprawled at the bottom of the ramped end of the platform, clutching his ankle and shaking his fist.

With a mental shrug, John set off for the front of the train.

John reached the end of the front carriage. He pulled down the window and stuck his head cautiously out.

Bright was still spreadeagled against the side of the engine, about seven metres in front of him. He was making little whimpering noises.

The train was gathering speed.

John cupped his hand around his mouth and

called, 'Erm . . . hello! Bright, it's me! Is there anything you'd like me to do?'

With great effort, Bright turned his head until he was facing John.

'Why yes, there is,' he said chirpily. 'You could go to the buffet and get us both a nice cup of coffee. Alternatively, and this is only a suggestion . . .' his face twisted with fury and he screamed, 'you could stop asking stupid questions and find a way to get me out of this mess!'

John gulped. 'OK. I'll go and . . .'

Bright's face became panic-stricken. 'Don't leave me!'

'But I've got to go and get help and . . .'

'Don't go anywhere. Stay there and think of something.' Bright's voice shook with self-pity. 'That would be just like you, rushing off and leaving a chap stuck to an engine, especially when it's all your fault; whose stupid idea was it to go to . . .' Bright's complaints tailed off. John was staring past him, his face a mask of horror.

'What's the matter with you now?' Bright demanded bitterly.

'I'm scared.'

'You're scared?! Who's stuck to this engine, you

or me? I'm the one who should be scared!'

'Yes, but I can see what's in front of this train.' John's head ducked back inside the carriage.

Bright struggled frantically to turn his head. 'What? What?'

The train went, 'Muuuuurrrrrmmmeeeeee.'

Bright screamed, 'Muuuuummmmyyyyyyy!'

The train shot into the tunnel.

*

It was a long tunnel.

When the train emerged into daylight, it took John several seconds to screw up the courage to stick his head back out of the window. It was an even bet whether he'd find that Bright had been scraped off the train, or whether . . . this thought made him feel very queasy . . . he had been smeared along the side of the train like a big fat insect hitting a car windscreen.

To his surprise, Bright was still there – and still alive judging by the amount of noise he was making.

'Hi there!' John waved cheerfully. 'Still hanging around then?'

Bright swore at John for nearly a minute without repeating himself once.

*

Market Biddleton wasn't the sort of place many trains stopped. This was fine by Ron Beasley, because Ron wasn't a very ambitious train-spotter.

While other train-spotters went haring off to far-flung stations to drool over exotic engines and rare rolling-stock, or bought expensive package holidays to travel on the Trans-Siberian Railway or the Orient Express, Ron was content to sit on the platform at Market Biddleton and watch the trains go by. He hadn't ticked many numbers off in his train-spotter's spotting book, but those he had ticked off he'd ticked off many, many times. The engines and coaches that went *whoosh* through Market Biddleton were like old friends. Besides, all the station staff knew Ron and he had his own seat in the station buffet.

As he sat on his favourite bench – just wondering whether to unzip his anorak a bit, because the day was getting quite warm – he heard the sound of an approaching train. Ron stood up, nodding to himself. Yes, that would be the 11.30 express to London; nine C class coaches pulled by the *City of Birkenhead*. He opened his book and licked the end of his pencil. Here it

came, a class 87 diesel-electric locomotive built by
the Crewe works in 1977, with a diesel engine
capable of delivering 21kV to two electric motors,
a top speed of 190kph, and a small boy stuck to
the side screaming his head off.

'Help, SOS, Mayday, oh no, I'm going to die . . .'

Ron stared at the train as it sped into the
distance. He looked down at his book.
Mechanically, he made a neat tick; then he looked
up again, and watched the train until it was out of
sight.

Ron scratched his head. He realized that his mouth was hanging open, and closed it. He thought for a moment or two more.

'Well, that's a first,' he said.

'Haven't you got *any* ideas?' howled Bright.

John scratched his head. Then he shook it.

'You're a useless twit, do you know that? You haven't got the brains God gave an electric toaster. Here am I, about to be splattered across the side of a train, and you just stand there like a useless great pile of . . .'

'I hate to interrupt,' said John, 'but have you noticed that since we passed through the last station there's been another railway line on our side of the train?'

'So what? Don't try to change the subject. You're a foolish, festering, feeble-minded, *why is there a track on this side? Does that mean what I think it means? Do something! Anything! Oh nooooooooo . . .*'

Miss Annabel Tinsel sat back in her seat and sighed happily. That nice Dr McNaughton had explained everything so clearly. He'd said it was perfectly normal for highly sensitive people to see things that other people couldn't, and only very ignorant and insensitive people would laugh at anyone who saw things like that. She felt so much better now. It was costing a fortune to go to London twice a week and see Dr McNaughton, but everyone said he was the best, and she had to admit it was money well spent. She was much calmer now, calmer than she had been before she started having . . . her visions. She had been such an old silly. She looked out of the window of her slow commuter train just as a faster train began to overtake it on the next line.

Yes, she felt so wonderfully relaxed. She could look out of the window secure in the knowledge that she wouldn't see any bug-eyed monsters or little green men or a *wild-eyed young boy wearing a frenzied expression and a torn jacket screaming horrible threats at her as he went past* . . .

Annabel Tinsel screamed and screamed and screamed . . .

Bright was looking very much the worse for wear.

'Cheer up,' John yelled from the carriage window, 'it could be worse!'

'Three tunnels!' howled Bright. 'Three! And two goods trains, and fourteen bridges! The last one nearly took my nose off. How could it possibly get worse?'

Something stung his cheek. And again. It felt like drops of water, hitting him very fast.

John gave him a feeble grin. 'Did you happen to read the weather forecast for today?'

The rain came down in buckets.

*

As the train pulled into the London terminus, a crowd of waiting passengers stared in open-mouthed wonder at the figure plastered to the side of the engine.

It was soaked through from head to foot. Its face was blackened by oil and streaked with tears. Its hair was standing on end. Its nose was running like a tap. Its jacket was torn. Its trousers were shredded. It was singing, in a croaking voice:

'Raindrops keep falling on my head;
I'm frozen s-s-s-stiff
And I wish that I was dead ...'

As the train came to rest and John waited impatiently for the doors to unlock, a railway official came across the platform. He approached the dripping scarecrow glued to the side of the engine, rubbing his eyes in disbelief.

'Good grief, laddie!' He stared at Bright. 'What happened to you?'

Bright gazed at him with eyes dulled with shock. John hurried over and explained what had happened.

The man shook his head in wonder. 'Well, that's incredible.' He looked up at Bright. 'You poor soul.' Tears welled in Bright's half-closed eyes at this display of human warmth. 'You've been stuck like that all the way from . . . where was it?'

John told him.

With a speed that would have made a champion gunslinger seethe with envy, the man reached behind his back and whipped out a ticket machine.

'Single or return?'

CHAPTER EIGHT

An Alarming Situation

Bright was still shaking with cold as he and John made their way up the steps to the Natural History Museum.

'I have a good mind to write to my MP about that ticket collector's attitude,' he grumbled. 'Either that or I'll get my father to have a word with some of his friends at MI6. They'll sort him out,' he muttered darkly.

John made a quick mental note not to get on the wrong side of Bright, and tried to change the subject. 'It's very impressive,' he exclaimed, pointing at the museum's grand entrance.

'Hmm.' Bright wasn't in the mood to appreciate

architecture. 'At least it's not made of metal,' he said sourly.

They trudged up the steps, through the large wooden doors and into the museum. They joined a line of people and began to queue.

'This way please,' ordered a museum guard. He was dressed in a smart blue uniform with bright shining buttons. The guard ushered people towards a small barrier. 'All bags to be checked and all metal objects to be placed on the side before you pass through. Thank you.'

Bright froze. He looked at the barrier. People were passing through a tall metal hoop.

'Oh no!' he muttered. 'Alarms!'

'Hurry along, please,' the guard called over to John and Bright. 'There are people waiting behind you.' He moved them smartly through the hoop.

John passed through without any trouble. Then it was Bright's turn.

BEEP! BEEP! BEEP! BEEP! BEEP! BEEP!

The alarm pierced the air. The queue of people behind Bright came to a sudden halt and stared. Bright began to colour with embarrassment.

The guard hurried over. 'Just stand there, young man, don't move, please. You've probably left some keys or something in your pockets.'

As the guard approached Bright, John thought he saw his uniform jacket twitch. What now? he wondered.

The guard patted Bright's pockets and seemed bemused. Then he began to run a metal stick up and down Bright.

BEEP! BEEP! BEEP! BEEP! BEEP! BEEP!

The portable detector went into a frenzy.

'Funny,' the guard muttered. 'Are you sure you haven't got any metal objects on you?'

'Not exactly *on* me,' muttered Bright.

The guard's jacket was still twitching as John walked over. He smiled winningly and tried to be helpful. 'Er, excuse me, I can explain. My friend is setting off the alarms because he's a magnet.'

The guard stared at John. For a long time. Then he gave a little half laugh. 'Oh, he's a magnet, is he? Of course he is! And do you know what I am?' He bent down and glared straight into John's eyes. 'I'm a fortune teller, I am. I can see into the future, and I predict that two little hooligans are going to get into very serious trouble for *fooling* about in the museum and telling *lies*!'

He took out his walkie-talkie and switched it on.

KKKKKKKKKKKKKK!

A blast of static screamed out of the radio set
and straight into the guard's ear. He yanked the
screeching radio away from his head, wincing with
pain, and twisted the 'off' knob savagely. He
glared at the malfunctioning walkie-talkie, then
turned back to Bright and narrowed his eyes.
'Right, that's it!' he barked. 'I don't know what's
going on, but I reckon you're playing some kind of

joke. Follow me!' He nodded towards a door that had a large sign on it saying SECURITY. 'Let's see what you're hiding!' He grabbed hold of Bright's shoulder.

PING!

The guard looked down at his jacket. One of his buttons had torn itself off and was now perched on Bright's nose.

'Oh no! Metal buttons!' groaned John.

PING! Another button ripped itself free.

PING! PING! PING! PING!

The guard stared at his flapping jacket, then transferred his astonished gaze towards Bright. The metal buttons had attached themselves to Bright in a perfectly straight line, starting at his nose and ending at his belly button.

John gawped as the stunned guard took of his jacket and examined it. Then he gasped with horror. Underneath his jacket, the guard was wearing braces. Braces with steel clips on the ends. To keep his trousers up.

John screwed his eyes shut and heard a *TWING*. A *TWANG* was followed quickly by a loud cry of despair.

He opened his eyes and saw the guard

struggling to hold up his trousers. His braces hung from Bright's left ear like a giant earring.

'Whatever it is, turn it off!' yelled the guard as he shuffled over to Bright and grabbed hold of the dangling straps of elastic.

'I can't!' cried out Bright. 'That's why I'm here!'

'Well, give me back my braces!' The guard began to pull at the braces with one hand whilst holding up his trousers with his other.

Bright grimaced in terror as the guard pulled the elastic taut. 'Don't let go!' he screamed.

By now a large crowd had stopped to watch the bizarre sight. John began to feel very embarrassed. 'Erm, I can explain everything,' he jabbered, flapping his arms nervously. 'He's a magnet! You see, we had a bit of an accident and Bright became magnetic and so we're here to see an expert who . . .' His feeble explanation tailed off as he realized that the crowd were more interested in the tug of war taking place before them.

The guard grimaced as he moved further and further away from Bright. The elastic stretched tighter and tighter. Something had to give. It did.

TWAAAAAAAANG!

The braces shot back across the room and hit the guard right on the nose. Everyone flinched.

The guard blinked. A stream of bright blood trickled from both his nostrils and began to drip on to his spotless shirt. His eyes streamed with tears.

'By *node*!' he moaned, snatching a handkerchief from his pocket and trying to staunch the flow. 'You'b bade by node bleed. Ooh, that *hurtf* . . .!'

Immediately, the crowd gathered round with helpful advice – 'Stick cotton wool up it . . .', 'Key down your back, that's what you need . . .', 'Try drinking a glass of water backwards . . .', 'No, that's hiccups . . .'

In the general mêlée, John felt someone tugging at his arm. It was Bright. 'Let's get out of here and find the professor,' he hissed.

John didn't need asking twice. The two boys scarpered out of the entrance hall and after spending a few moments disposing of the guard's buttons, they made their way to the museum's information desk. An official-looking woman was sitting behind a computer terminal. John stepped forward.

'We've come to see Professor Brayn. My name is John Watt and this is my friend Vernon Bright.'

'Watt, did you say?'

'I said, we're here to see Professor Brayn,' replied John.

The woman stared hard at him. 'I know that! I was asking if your name was Watt.'

John smiled. 'Oh I see. You were saying "Watt" when I thought you were saying "what".'

'What?'

John rolled his eyes. 'Twenty-four,' he muttered to Bright.

The woman tapped at her computer keyboard. 'The professor is in today,' she said. 'Is he expecting you?'

'Er, yes,' lied John. He made a grab for Bright and pulled him next to the desk.

Bright pushed John's arm away. 'What are you playing at?'

As Bright came close to it, the computer immediately gave a high-pitched squeal and the screen went dead. John jerked his head towards it, keeping his eyes on Bright. Understanding John's ruse, Bright gave an angry shrug.

The woman gave the computer a slap that probably wasn't recommended in the Owner's Manual. 'Huh! Crashed again!'

John put on his best smile. 'Perhaps if you just let us know what room he's in, we'll make our own way there.'

'You're sure he's expecting you?' she asked again, eyeing them suspiciously.

'Oh yes, I'm certain,' John replied, nodding.

Grudgingly, the woman gave them a floor plan of the museum.

'You'll find the professor on this floor. His offices are in the Reserve Collection Department.' She took a highlighter and marked the route they were to follow.

As Bright moved away from the desk, the computer pinged back into life. The woman shook her head. 'Technology,' she muttered under her breath, and gave the computer a final thump for good luck and for the trouble it brought to her life.

Minutes later, they stood in front of an office door. An official-looking sign on the door said, 'Professor B. G. Brayn.' A less official-looking sign below it said, *You don't have to be a demented crackpot to work here, but it helps.*

At John's tentative knock, the door was flung open by a large bearded man who glared suspiciously at the two boys. 'Yes?' he rasped. Then the sign on the door caught his eye. He immediately turned brick red, tore the sign off the door, crumpled it and thrust it behind his back, apparently in an attempt to pretend that it had never been there in the first place.

John said nervously, 'Er . . . we've got a bit of a problem to do with magnetism . . .'

The professor's eyebrows shot up. 'Ahh? And you've come to see me? Good decision.'

John remembered his manners. 'I'm Watt,' he told the professor, 'and he's Bright.'

'Well, well, well!' The professor's eyes twinkled. 'Watt a Bright pair you are! Ha ha ha!'

Bright shut his eyes and groaned. 'One thousand, three hundred.'

'Watt, Bright, ha ha! Just a little joke.'

'Microscopic,' agreed Bright.

'Er, yes.' The professor coughed. 'Well, now, what seems to be the problem?'

They told him. This took some time.

When they had finished, the professor was gazing at them with a curiously blank expression. 'So, let me make sure I understand this correctly.' He pointed at Bright. 'Unless I'm mistaken, you think you're a magnet.'

As if in reply, the professor's pen flicked out of

his top pocket, leapt through the air and thudded into Bright's ear.

The professor looked quizzical, and then amazed as his glasses shot off his nose and attached themselves to Bright's upper lip.

'Now that is interesting,' said the professor as he removed his possessions from Bright's head. 'I wonder . . .'

He disappeared into the next room. There was a sound of drawers opening and frantic rummaging, then the professor came back holding a short metal bar, silver at one end and red at the other.

'Now, let's see . . .'

He held the metal bar vertically over Bright's head with the red end pointing downwards. It quivered in his grasp, but seemed to be hovering, as if unwilling to come into contact with Bright's head.

'Aha!' said the professor. 'So that must mean . . .'

He turned the magnet over so that the silver end was pointing downwards. It immediately thudded down on to Bright's skull.

'Ow!' Bright rubbed his stinging scalp and looked daggers at the beaming professor.

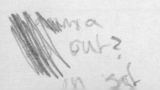

'There we are then,' said the professor happily.

John scratched his head. 'Where are we?'

'Your friend has all the characteristics of a bar magnet.' The professor held up the metal bar. 'This is a conventional bar magnet. The red end is its north pole, the silver end its south pole. Now, a north pole will attract a south pole, but repel another north pole, and a south pole will attract a north pole, but repel another south pole . . .'

John felt his head beginning to spin. 'Sorry?'

The professor clicked his tongue irritably. 'It's very simple. Different poles attract each other, the same poles repel each other. So, when I hold the red end of the magnet, the north pole, over your friend's head, his magnetic field repels it; whereas if I hold the *silver* end over his head . . .'

'Ow!'

'The head attracts it, proving that your friend's head is his magnetic north pole, which would lead us naturally to conclude that his feet are his south pole.' The professor pocketed the bar magnet. 'Actually, the north pole should be called the north-seeking pole, because if you held the magnet on a piece of string or something, that end would turn north . . .'

'Like a compass needle.'

'Exactly.' The professor looked a little put-out at being interrupted. Then he brightened again. 'This is really extraordinarily interesting.'

'Interesting? It's unnatural,' said John.

'Well, it's certainly unusual,' said the professor. 'Electricity occurs naturally in all living things, and when an electric current flows, it creates a magnetic field. In the human body, for instance, your nerve impulses constantly send electric messages . . .'

'Yes, yes, I know all that,' said Bright.

The professor gave him a disapproving look. 'However, that can't be what's making you magnetic. If you'd used the electrical impulses in your body to turn yourself into some sort of bio-electromagnet, the magnetic field would be constantly changing – or else your nerves and muscles would have stopped working. You'd be dead.'

Bright turned even paler than before.

'Since you're clearly not dead,' the professor went on cheerfully, 'another possibility is that you've managed to magnetize all the iron in your body. That shouldn't be possible for at least three reasons. One,' the professor ticked off the points on his fingers, 'most of the iron in your body is constantly moving about (in your red blood cells, for instance) and if it became magnetized it would clump together. Two, you don't have enough iron in your body to create such a powerful effect. And three, bits of you would be attracted to other bits of you. Your head should be attracted to your feet, so that if you bent over . . . well, it'd make biting your toenails a whole lot easier, that's for sure.'

John stared at the professor. 'So why didn't any of that happen?'

The professor rubbed his hands gleefully. 'I don't know. Whatever is going on must be more complicated than we think.' He pulled something that looked like a hospital trolley away from the wall, and began undoing straps. 'Just hop on here, will you?'

Bright eyed these preparations with mounting alarm. 'What are you going to do?'

'You want to find out what's happened to you, don't you?' The professor turned towards him with an odd look on his face. 'So do I.'

Bright began to back away. 'Well, it's been very interesting, but I think we'd better be going now . . .'

The professor shook his head. He reached into his pocket and pulled out a key. 'I don't think so,' he said softly. 'I couldn't possibly let you go now.' He gave a smile that made John's blood run cold. 'Not until . . .'

'Not until . . . ?' Bright squeaked.

The professor began to walk slowly towards Bright. 'Not until you've helped me with my experiments.'

CHAPTER NINE

'Just stay there.' The professor had a mad glint in his eye.

Bright looked worried. 'Experiments?' he said nervously. 'What sort of experiments?'

'Don't worry,' said the professor breezily. 'They won't hurt a bit.'

No, they'll probably hurt a lot! thought John. After his recent experiences, he took what scientists said about the effects of their experiments with a large sackful of salt.

Professor Brayn moved towards the door. 'I'll just get my assistants.' As he left the room, Bright swore he could hear the professor muttering to himself about winning the Nobel prize and being more famous than Einstein.

The professor closed the door. Half a second later, there was a clicking noise.

Bright and John looked at each other in horror. As one, they rushed to the door and wrestled with the handle.

'He's locked us in!' screamed Bright. 'I don't believe it!' He shook the handle violently.

'There's no point doing that, the door's locked,' said John.

'I know,' replied Bright angrily, 'but it's a steel handle. I'm stuck to it!'

John helped pull Bright away from the door handle. 'We need to think about this logically,' he mused and began to pace up and down the room in a Sherlock-Holmes-like manner. After a few seconds, he threw up his hands in triumph. 'I know! You could be like James Bond! He uses special gadgets to unlock doors. You can use your special power to unlock this door!'

Bright stared at John. 'Oh, *very* logical,' he said sarcastically. 'Unfortunately, I'm not a special 007 spy gadget, I'm a magnet!'

John was crestfallen. 'Well, have you got any bright ideas?'

'One thousand, three hundred and one,' snarled Bright. 'And don't apologize, I'm not in the mood.'

The boys sat in silence for some time, before John gave a large sigh. 'It looks as though you're just going to have to let the professor carry out his experiments.'

Bright shook his head. 'What gives Professor Brayn the right to do his experiments on me?'

'I've heard something like that before,' said John pointedly. Bright looked puzzled. 'Horace. Remember?' prompted John.

The penny dropped. 'But that's different,' protested Bright.

Before John could ask in *what* way it was different, the door opened and the professor marched in. With him were two white-coated assistants. They looked brisk and efficient and stared at Bright in eager anticipation. Behind them stood another security guard, blocking the doorway. Bright gulped.

'Here's our specimen,' announced the professor. The assistants were positively drooling. Like vampires at a feast, thought John. The assistants and guard moved towards Bright and surrounded him.

'Now, what shall we start with?' wondered the professor.

Bright's lower lip began to quiver. John had to do something. He couldn't let Bright become the subject of an experiment. He looked around, wishing that he could suddenly come up with a brilliant idea.

He did.

Underneath the professor's desk, a metal bin caught his eye. He picked it up.

'Bright!' he shouted. Bright turned. The bin flew out of John's hands and cut through the air as it headed towards Bright. The professor, assistants and security guard all instinctively ducked to avoid the flying object.

'RUN!' yelled John. He grabbed Bright and shot past the group of startled adults, through the door and into the corridor.

'Which way?' shouted Bright.

'I don't know, just keep running!' John skidded off down the shiny corridor. Bright charged after him. The guard, professor and assistants had recovered their senses and were now in close pursuit.

'STOP!' yelled the guard. He made a lunge for

the boys and slipped on the highly polished floor.

'Come baaackaagghhh!' The assistants and the professor went flying as they crashed into the guard's sprawled body.

Bright and John took their opportunity and hurtled down a flight of stairs. Other museum visitors were sent spinning as they tried to avoid the two 'hooligans', one of whom had a waste paper bin attached to the side of his face.

Minutes later, John and Bright ran into a large gallery and pressed themselves against the wall.

'I think we've shaken them off,' John panted. 'I wonder where we are?' He looked up. Massive skeletons towered above them. The Dinosaur Gallery! John recognized several of the huge creatures from his *Big Book of Big Dinosaurs*: Diplodocus, Stegosaurus and Tyrannosaurus rex stood majestically in the centre of the gallery.

Above them, Pterodactyls appeared to be flying, although in reality they were attached to the ceiling by chains.

Incredible! John momentarily forgot about the chase and gazed in awe at the skeleton monsters that once walked the earth millions of years ago.

'Amazing!' he sighed. 'How are the skeletons held together?' he asked Bright.

'Simple,' replied Bright. 'By clips, screws and staples.' He paused. His stomach began to churn.

John's stomach joined in the churning. 'Would the clips, screws and staples be made out of metal . . . ?' John asked, although he already knew the answer.

Bright nodded slowly and stared at the exhibits. Above him, the Pterodactyls began to swing on their metal chains. Bright's jaw dropped. The

Tyrannosaurus rex was trying to free itself! He spun round. Every dinosaur in the gallery was moving!

Other visitors in the museum began to scream in terror as the skeletons shook violently. Bones began to clatter and fall to the floor as the screws and bars that held the skeletons together twisted and bent in an effort to free themselves and attach themselves to Bright.

'Get out of here!' ordered Bright. John nodded wordlessly. He shot for the exit as the skeletons shook themselves to pieces, leaving mounds of bones. That's what doggy heaven must be like, was John's last thought as he careered out of the gallery. Behind him he could hear a clattering and crashing as the work of a hundred years of careful preservation and construction, and several hundred million years of evolution, was destroyed in seconds flat.

'OI! YOU TWO!'

Bright and John didn't wait to find out who wanted them now; they made a mad dash for the museum's exit. The whole place was a mass of confusion. Alarms clanged, sirens wailed and people seemed to be either trying to grab hold of them or get out of their way. Amidst all the madness, Bright and John finally burst through the exit barrier, hurtled down the museum steps and ran off as quickly as they could.

They carried on charging through the streets for a long time, bumping into people, crashing into concrete pillars, turning left, right, left again, straight on, or anywhere, just to get well away from the museum, the pile of bones and the professor. But even in the mad dash, John kept a close eye on his magnetized friend, making sure he kept himself between Bright and any passing buses or cars that might whisk him away.

Eventually, John saw an entrance to one of London's parks. 'In there!' he cried. 'We can take a rest.'

Bright was too exhausted to do anything but agree. He staggered after John, and followed him to the side of a lake where the two boys collapsed on the ground and tried to get air into their aching lungs. John pulled the waste paper bin off the side of Bright's face and hurled it towards the lake. The basket swerved in mid-air and came back like a boomerang.

'Ow!'

'Whoops!' John pulled the bin off Bright again. He tried not to grin at Bright's injured look as he carried it away to a safe distance.

'So where are we?' Bright asked miserably.

There was a pointed silence.

'Brilliant,' moaned Bright. 'We're lost.'

'We're not lost,' John snapped back. 'I just don't know where we are.'

'Oh, well, that's all right then,' Bright sneered.

John peered into the distance. 'I know the railway station is in north London.' He paused. 'But I'm not sure which way north is,' he added lamely.

Bright raised an eyebrow. 'We need to know which way north is?'

John nodded.

'All right . . . go and hire a boat.' Bright pointed at a line of rowing boats floating on the water's edge.

John wondered what Bright was going on about. How would hiring a boat help? What did he intend to do, row home? He shook his head. 'I haven't got any money left. I'm all spent up on the train fare.'

Bright gave a sigh, stood up and began to walk into the lake.

John jumped up. Surely Bright wasn't going to try and drown himself! 'Don't do it, Bright! I know you're upset, but I'm sure we can talk about this ... Don't be stupid!' he called out, rushing to the water's side.

Bright turned to John. 'I am NEVER stupid,' he said. 'I am trying to find out which way we should go to get back to the train station!'

John looked on in astonishment as Bright lay flat in the water and began to float. After a moment or two, he began to slowly spin round.

After a few more seconds of twitching and turning, Bright found himself with his head pointing out across the lake.

'Are you all right?' asked John, wondering if the magnetism had done serious damage to Bright's brain. 'What are you doing?'

'I'm a compass. My head's pointing towards magnetic north and my feet arc facing magnetic south. Take a line of which way my head is pointing. Line it up with a landmark or something. It'll be near enough. We can then head towards it.'

John followed the line of Bright's head. Across

the lake and way beyond the park, he could make out a tall red-brick building, with a dome on top.

'The station!' he cried. 'I remember it!'

Bright stood up and waded back to shore. He was soaking wet. Again.

John gazed at the dripping figure of Bright. 'You know, Bright, that was incredibly clever.'

Bright shrugged his shoulders. 'Well, you know how it is.'

'I am so impressed,' continued John. 'I'd never have thought of doing that.'

Bright looked smug. 'Of course you wouldn't. Nobody but me would have thought of it.'

'You're not wrong there.' John nodded wisely. 'In fact, do you know, if I'd wanted to know where the station was, I'm so stupid, I'd have just asked someone?'

John walked off, giggling to himself, leaving a dripping Bright staring after him and feeling very foolish.

CHAPTER TEN

Any Old Iron . . .?

The train journey back had been a nightmare.

At the station, Bright had been accused of trying to steal the fourteen baggage trolleys and their contents that had swooped down on him as soon as he entered the concourse. In the train, every time the refreshments trolley came past it had made a determined attempt to climb into Bright's lap. One man trying to do the crossword suddenly found his steel pen jerked from his fingers; after John had pulled it out of Bright's left nostril and handed it back, the man seemed to have lost all interest in the crossword.

John had spent the entire journey handing back keys, pens and other metallic objects to their outraged owners, and apologizing to people whose mobile phones and laptops wouldn't work. By the time they finally staggered out of the station, John was feeling pretty frazzled and Bright was on the verge of collapse.

Bright crumpled on to a wooden bench on the station forecourt. He waved an arm pathetically at John. 'I'm finished. Go. Leave me.'

John was too tired to be sympathetic. 'Come on, we've got to get you home.'

'I'll never make it.' Bright buried his head in his shoulder and snuffled.

'I shall just sit here until I die and it's all your fault.'

'Oh yes?' John had had about enough. 'All right, it was my fault! It was my fault that you got magnetized instead of a poor little guinea pig who never did you any harm and wouldn't even have been able to understand what was happening to it when it stuck to the side of its cage and couldn't get off, and do you know what? I'm glad that was my fault.' He turned on his heel and walked away.

'Wait!' Bright's wail brought John up short. Unwillingly, he turned and went back to the

huddled figure on the bench. After a few more snuffles, Bright pulled himself together and looked at John. His face was so bleak and hopeless that John couldn't help feeling sorry for him again.

Bright sat forward, put his elbows on his knees, and stared at the floor. 'I just never thought. I never wanted to do anything nasty to Horace. I just wanted to find out if my machine worked. My dad always says that sacrifices have to be made in the name of science.'

John could have pointed out that people who

said things like that were never the ones making the sacrifices, but he kept the thought to himself.

Bright wiped his nose on his sleeve and went on. 'But you're right. I know what it's like now. I know what it's like to have terrible things happening to you that you can't control, and I promise you this . . .' He turned back to John and his eyes burned with sincerity. 'I promise you that I will never again hurt a living thing in my experiments. And I want to thank you for sticking by me.' Bright stuck his hand out. Wordlessly, John shook it. 'Thank you, John. You're a real friend.'

After that, they sat in silence for a while.

'I've been thinking,' said John.

'Hah!' Bright bit his lip. 'Sorry, sorry. Force of habit. Go on, please.'

'Well, you know what the professor said about an electric current creating a magnetic field . . . ?'

'Yes. That's how electricity is generated, you know, by spinning magnets inside coils of wire to set up electric currents. And if you do it the opposite way round – if you wrap insulated wire around an iron core, and put a current through the wire – the iron becomes an electromagnet. That's what they use in scrapyards for moving old cars and stuff about.'

'And when you switch the current off, the iron stops being magnetic?'

'Yes. If you want to shift an old car, you use a crane to put the electromagnet over the car and switch it on. It picks up the car . . .' Bright raised one hand, palm down to represent the magnet lifting the car and moved it down the bench. 'You move the car to where you want it, switch the magnet off and splat!' He slammed his hand down on to the bench.

John nodded excitedly. 'Right. So, if it's the iron in your body that's making you magnetic, could you use an electromagnet to . . .'

'To wipe out my magnetic field?' Bright snapped bolt upright and snapped his fingers. 'That's brilliant!'

John stared at him. 'Oh. Is it?'

'It might just work. Electromagnets are very powerful. If you put an electromagnet too close to a videotape, it'll wipe what you've recorded off the magnetic tape.'

'So whatever your machine did to you, an electromagnet could reverse it?'

127

'It *might*.' Bright stood up and squared his shoulders. 'Of course, there's only one way to find out.'

John scrambled to his feet. 'What's that?'

'To try it.' Bright set off down the street.

'Where are we going?'

Without breaking stride, Bright turned to John. 'To Dodgy Dave's – OW!'

'Tell you what,' said John, rolling his sleeves up, 'let's walk on the other side of the street, shall we? The side across from the park. Where there aren't any iron railings?'

'Mffulgurg,' agreed Bright.

Dodgy Dave stared at John. 'You want me to do *what*?'

John sighed. 'I told you. Something's happened to Bright . . .'

'Who?'

'Bright . . . Vernon Bright . . . er – Vernie?'

'Oh, the screwball.'

Explaining the situation to Dave took some time, mostly because John was still pretty unclear on the details himself. He'd volunteered to go and enlist Dave's help because Bright didn't dare come into the yard, bristling as it was with nearly-ex-military hardware.

'So, let's get this straight,' drawled Dave slowly after John had explained the situation for the fourth time. 'You want the electromagnet I use for moving my merchandise around the yard.' He stuck his fingers through the mesh of his string vest and scratched his belly reflectively. 'You want your buddy, Bright, who is a magnet at this moment in time, on account of some cockamamie experiment he was doing, to stand under it. Then you want me to switch it on.'

John nodded eagerly. Dave sighed.

'And folk hereabouts reckon *I'm* weird.' He mused for a moment. Then he shrugged. 'What the heck, it's got to be more fun than watching TV. Wheel him in.'

'He'll do it,' John reported to Bright, 'but there's a problem.'

Bright eyed John warily. 'And that is?'

'His electromagnet is on a crane that runs on tracks, yeah?' Bright nodded. 'It only goes so far towards the gate. You'll have to come into the yard to get underneath it, or it won't work.'

Bright shuddered. 'But that yard is full of metal. Ammo boxes, spare parts, scrap . . .'

'I know.'

'. . . rusty tools, rolls of barbed wire, chains . . .'

'There's no other way. I've marked a cross on the ground under where the magnet is. If you can get to that cross, Dave will do the rest.'

Bright gave John a cornered look. Then he bit his lip. 'All right.'

'I'll go with you,' said John bravely.

Bright shook his head. 'No point in both of us getting smashed to bits. I've got to do this by myself.'

John peered through the gate. From his place by the crane's controls, Dave gave him the thumbs up. John turned back to Bright. 'He's ready.'

'Right.' Bright grasped John's shoulder. 'If this doesn't work . . . if I don't make it . . .' He cleared his throat. 'Promise me . . . promise me you'll look after Horace.'

John nodded, overcome. 'I will, Bright.'

'All right. Here goes nothing . . .'

Bright turned . . .

. . . and started his run.

*

To John, whose nerves were twanging like an over-tightened guitar string, everything that followed seemed to happen in slow motion.

A sudden silence fell, through which John swore he could hear the beating of his own heart. Time ran like treacle as Bright's feet pounded towards the yard, kicking up little spurts of dust with every step.

He reached the gateway. Even though the gates were firmly pinned back, they rattled and shook

like giant jaws struggling to snap shut and chop Bright in two.

Then Bright's magnetic field started to operate on Dave's 'merchandise'.

Bits of surplus hardware began to leap at Bright, who was now running blind with his hands and arms held across his head to protect himself. Like a film of an explosion played in reverse, bits of iron and steel shrapnel flew through the air to fasten themselves on to the desperately running figure. Nuts and bolts of all sizes, radio aerials, bits of loose chain and motor spares shot towards Bright like angry bees swarming round an enemy. In steel mesh crates, more pieces of military junk rattled and leapt against their bars like small vicious animals thirsting for Bright's blood.

Bright ran on, staggering now. John followed along in his wake, shouting encouragement: 'Go on, Bright, nearly there! Just a few more steps . . .'

But the shower of items shooting towards Bright had become a cloud. John could hardly see the struggling figure through the streams of flying metal. Dave stood by the crane controls, with his mouth wide open, and his moustache bristling in astonishment, as the figure of Bright became a huge, distorted mass, only vaguely human-shaped, like a horribly deformed robot.

The figure lurched on for a few more leaden steps, then stopped.

John waved his arms about, screaming at the top of his lungs, 'Bright! You're almost under the crane!' His voice was almost drowned in the metallic clatter of yet more junk slamming into the terrible, pitiful iron creature that his friend had become. 'You're almost there! Three more steps! Keep going, do you hear me? Keep going!'

Incredibly, despite its coating of iron and steel that must have weighed hundreds of kilograms, the figure responded. One dragging, pain-filled step ... two ... three ... and Bright stood in the centre of the cross, directly under the swaying electromagnet. John turned towards Dave, cupped his hands around his mouth, and screamed, 'NOW!!!'

Dave hit the power switch.

The magnet came to life with a deep electric hum. A line of blue electric fire shot from the rim of the magnet to the figure beneath. The line became a web, skidding and crawling across the magnet, the iron monster and the air between. Iron and steel fragments began to lift away from Bright in a feverish dance. John threw himself to the ground just in time as the air all around became a whirlwind of flying metal. The hum of the magnet became a whine and climbed in pitch until it was a white-hot scream in John's ears. The air tasted like tin.

An explosion of sound battered John's ears; a blinding flash of light burned through his closed eyelids. Then there was silence.

Slowly, cautiously, John looked up.

The yard looked as if a bomb had hit it, which was very nearly the case. The blast had sent pieces of iron and steel shooting in all directions. All the windows in the main warehouse were smashed. Several bits of junk had embedded themselves in the wooden doors. Something had nearly embedded itself in Dave, but in the end had merely whipped the top of his hat off.

John looked up. The electromagnet hung swaying from its crane. It was smoking.

He looked down. Bright lay in a crumpled heap. He was smoking too.

Slowly, Bright pulled himself into a sitting position. His expression was shocked. His hair

134

stood on end. Bits of it, and his clothing, smouldered gently. He ran his hands carefully over his body, wincing when he touched an especially sore bit. Then he looked up at John with a face filled with wonder.

'It worked?' asked John, in hushed tones.

Bright reached out and picked up a steel spanner. He opened his hand. The spanner fell to the floor.

'It worked,' he said in a whisper.

John threw back his head and punched the air in triumph. 'Yeeeehaa! Result! Sorted! Job done!'

Bright's shoulders shook. John wasn't sure if he was laughing or crying. Probably both, he decided.

Dodgy Dave came over, walking like a man in a dream. He stood beside them, surveying the chaos. Then he took his hat off and pushed his arm through the hole in the crown. He waggled his fingers about, staring at them in wonder.

John began to feel awkward. 'Sorry about the mess,' he said uneasily.

Dave suddenly threw back his head with a great bellow of laughter. He clapped John on the shoulder. 'Don't make no never-mind. I ain't never seen anything like that in all my born days.' He

waved a hand vaguely at the yard. 'Insurance'll cover this. I remember one time some dad-blasted fool left a live round in a mortar I got sent. You should've seen the mess *that* caused.' He chuckled nostalgically. 'You guys run along now. I'm going to ring the boys from the Line Dancing Club and tell them all about what happened here.' He waved at them and wandered unsteadily off, still chuckling.

In silence, Bright and John left the yard.

As they walked back towards Bright's house, John thought about everything that had happened over the past week. Coming to a new school had been a lot more eventful than he'd bargained for. He'd found a friend. He'd also discovered that science could be very interesting, not to mention hair-raising.

At Bright's gate, they paused.

Bright stopped with his hand on the gate, and turned to John. He was clearly embarrassed.

'Erm . . . about the past couple of days,' he said awkwardly. 'You . . . er . . . won't tell anybody at school, will you? They might think it was funny.'

John struggled to keep a straight face. 'I suppose they might,' he said. 'No, I won't say anything.'

Relief flooded Bright's face. 'Good. Good. And I promise you, I really have learnt my lesson from all this. I understand now that you can't just rush about doing experiments. You have to think about the consequences. And I promise you that from now on, I'll always think very carefully about the effects of my experiments before I do them. Shake on it?' He thrust his hand out.

Smiling, John took it.

There was a buzz, and a crackle. John snapped to attention, his eyes wide with shock. His hair stood on end, his teeth clenched, his body jerked.

With a gasp, Bright snatched his hand away.

The two bedraggled, shock-headed figures gazed at each other in horror. Bright stared at the hand he had offered John, and gave a moan of despair.

The electromagnet had cured him – very nearly.

Bright wasn't magnetic any more.

He was electric!